Sophie's eyes ___ *sexy. Her complexion* ___ *perfect. Her lips plump, kissable. Jeb's heart speeded up, scrambling his pulse.*

He told himself to pull away and get the hell out. But he didn't move. Didn't speak. Barely breathed. Not because she was so pretty, or even because she was suddenly so close. But because she had the same look of confusion on her face that he was sure was on his.

Her baby yelped, and Jeb jumped as if someone had exploded a firecracker. He grabbed his files and headed for the door without a word. What could he say? *I nearly made the biggest mistake of my life and kissed you?* An employee? A woman with a baby? He couldn't believe he'd almost kissed her. How would he ever explain it to the woman who looked as confused by the attraction as he was?

Dear Reader,

This is a special year for Harlequin. Imagine, sixty years!

It's a privilege to be one of their authors. Harlequin has survived the trends through a commitment to providing the very best stories for readers. In the years I've published with them, I've witnessed and lived through several incarnations of the types of stories published by the individual lines. But without a doubt, Harlequin's top priority through it all has been quality stories. They know readers are passionate about wonderful romances and they work to provide them!

It's also my pleasure to have *Maid in Montana* counted among the books published by Harlequin. This story of a strong hero who's determined to overcome his problems alone, and who can't resist helping the heroine, is one of my personal favorites. Jeb and Sophie are fun people who aren't merely passionate about each other; they're passionate about life. Their story will make you laugh and cry!

Have a wonderful summer! Pick up an extra book or two for the beach or whatever summer hideaway you choose!

Susan Meier

SUSAN MEIER

Maid in Montana

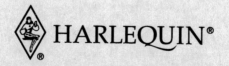

TORONTO • NEW YORK • LONDON
AMSTERDAM • PARIS • SYDNEY • HAMBURG
STOCKHOLM • ATHENS • TOKYO • MILAN • MADRID
PRAGUE • WARSAW • BUDAPEST • AUCKLAND

Recycling programs
for this product may
not exist in your area.

ISBN-13: 978-0-373-18449-1

MAID IN MONTANA

First North American Publication 2009.

Copyright © 2009 by Linda Susan Meier.

www.eHarlequin.com

Printed in U.S.A.

Susan Meier spent most of her twenties thinking she was a job-hopper—until she began to write and realized everything that had come before was only research! As one of eleven children, with twenty-four nieces and nephews and three kids of her own, Susan has had plenty of real-life experience watching romance blossom in unexpected ways. She lives in western Pennsylvania with her wonderful husband, Mike, three children, and two overfed, well-cuddled cats, Sophie and Fluffy. You can visit Susan's Web site at www.susanmeier.com.

Susan brings you a special treat this Christmas in
The Magic of a Family Christmas
November 2009

Do you ever wish you could
step into someone else's shoes?

Now you can with Harlequin Romance®.
Our new miniseries is brimming with contemporary,
feel-good stories.

Our modern-day Cinderellas
swap glass slippers for stylish stilettos!

So follow each footstep from makeover to marriage,
rags to riches, as these women
fulfill their hopes and dreams....

**Next month step into Cassidy's shoes
to find out if this L.A. Cinderella
meets a movie-star-gorgeous prince in:**

His L.A. Cinderella
by
Trish Wylie

CHAPTER ONE

JEB WORTHINGTON watched the aging sport utility vehicle chug up the tree-lined road leading to his ranch. He pulled on his horse's reins, stopping Jezebel, and reached for his small binoculars.

Yep. Just as he suspected. His new housekeeper, Sophie Penazzi, had arrived.

Adjusting the glasses, he watched her get out of the car, taking in her straight, shoulder-length brown hair that, if he remembered correctly, was a color almost identical to the dark brown of her eyes.

She stretched, working the kinks out of her back and shoulders from the long drive. The smooth, even tan of her skin brought visions of her in a bikini, rushing into the crashing waves of the Pacific, surfboard under her arm. It didn't surprise him that he'd envision her that way. Not only did her résumé list her home as Malibu, but also there was a part of him that would pay very good money to see her perfect bottom in a bikini.

He dropped the glasses to his thigh. Those were exactly the kinds of things he could not—*would not*—think about his new housekeeper. He'd lost the last one because she'd made a pass at him and he'd fired her. But instead of admitting she'd been let go because she'd tried to use her position as a springboard to becoming mistress of the house, Maria had promptly gone into town and trashed his reputation, claiming she'd quit because he was a grouch, too difficult to work for. The only way he'd recoup his standing with the locals would be to be nice to this new housekeeper, proving Maria had lied.

But being nice came with trouble of its own. Or maybe better said: Being nice to a live-in employee came with rules of its own. A line had to be drawn. He didn't want to be accused of sexual harassment or even flirting. And he wouldn't. He'd find a middle ground.

He nudged Jezebel, urging her to increase her pace.

Sophie bent into the rear compartment of her SUV. After setting several suitcases on the ground behind her vehicle, she lifted out an odd looking thing covered in net, at least four feet long and flat as a pancake. From the brackets on the side, he suspected that whatever it was, it was folded up. God only knew what it became when she unfolded it.

Once again, he nudged Jezebel, this time increasing her walk to a trot.

Adjusting the glasses so he could watch her as he rode, he saw Sophie slam the rear hatch, open the back door and bend inside.

There was more?

She pulled out a small seat and what looked to be a cooler and Jeb took Jezebel to a full gallop. What the hell was this woman doing? Planning to take over a wing of his house? Sure, she had to live with him, but he remembered telling her that her quarters were a bedroom, sitting room and a bathroom. She didn't get to spread out all over his home.

He galloped past the outbuildings and barn, slowing Jezebel when they neared the driveway and taking her down to a walk when they reached the pavement.

Obviously hearing the clip-clop of Jez's approach, Sophie turned around. Shading her eyes with her hand, she looked up at him and called, "Hey! Good morning."

Her bright brown eyes shone with joy, accenting her pert little nose, wide smile and nicely defined chin. He should have kept his eyes on her face, but the blue top clinging to her breasts and the jeans outlining her perfect bottom drew his gaze downward until he'd taken in every feminine inch of her.

Irritated with himself, he nearly cursed. Why had he hired someone so cute?

A glance at her mountain of gear only increased his ire. Obviously she was all wrong for this job. He reined Jez a few feet ahead of the car, and growled, "What are you—"

Too late. Sophie ducked into her back seat again and Jeb stopped talking. Not only was she providing him with a jaw-dropping view of her backside, but also there was little sense talking when his conversation partner couldn't hear him.

He waited patiently, ready to ask her just how much junk she thought she could get into a small suite of rooms, but when she pulled out of the back seat, baby in her arms, the words he'd intended to say fell out of his head. He was—for the first time ever—speechless.

She smiled at him. "I'm sorry. What did you say?"

He stared at her. Then the baby. The kid was small, but chubby. Healthy. With pink cheeks and a thatch of thick black hair that poked out in all directions.

The only thing that came out of his mouth was, "What are you doing?"

She frowned. "You said move in. Today. So I can start working tomorrow. Did I misread your instructions?"

"Apparently! Since I don't remember telling you to bring a baby!"

"Oh!" She laughed. "This is my son. Brady." She kissed the little boy's cheek. "Say hello, Brady."

The baby cooed and gooed and Jeb's heart stuttered in his chest. Willing back the swell of emotions that threatened to overtake him, he simply said, "You can't have a baby here."

Sophie kissed the baby's cheek again. "Why not? The agency said it wasn't a problem."

"The employment agency told you that you could bring him?"

"Yes, when they explained that this job was for a live-in housekeeper, I told them about Brady and they said it was no problem for me to bring him."

"I gave them the exact opposite instruction! I said, *no kids*." Somebody's head was going to roll.

"What difference does it make?" she asked cheerfully before she ran her fingers through her baby's unruly dark hair, trying to tame it. "I'm not working 24/7. Only eight or ten hours a day. And not all back-to-back hours. You said that on my interview. Since my work requires feeding you supper…which takes us past a five o'clock quitting time, especially cleaning up the dining room and kitchen after you eat, you said my days are pretty much my own. I can organize them any way I want. And that means I have plenty of time to care for Brady."

"I can't have a baby here!"

Her expression hardened. Her shiny brown eyes turned into laser beams of steely determination. The laughter was gone from her voice when she said, "Mr. Worthington, obviously there was a mess-up at the agency, but that doesn't mean we can't make the best of it."

Jezebel danced from foot to foot. A clear sign that Jeb's agitation was transmitting itself to her. He took a breath and spoke more calmly. "I don't want to make the best of it. I have clients coming—"

Jezebel danced around some more. Jeb tugged lightly on the reins, knowing he had to get her to the stable before he could finish this conversation. "Don't move. I'll be back."

He rode Jezebel into the stable, slid off the saddle and tossed the reins to a hand who was mucking stalls. "Take care of her."

With the anger in his belly churning into hurricane force, he strode outside again and to the driveway. Sophie Penazzi stood beside her vehicle, her child sitting in the plastic basket thing, her arms crossed on her chest.

"I want a thousand dollars to pay for the cost of this trip."

He stopped a few feet in front of her. "A thousand dollars?"

"It should be three. I let my apartment go." Her voice wobbled, but she paused, drew in a breath and very strongly said, "I paid to put my things in storage. I also have the expenses of traveling here. It's cost me a lot to take this job, and if I'm not staying, then I want to be reimbursed." She caught his gaze. "Now."

"We have an employment agreement.

You're staying," Jeb said, holding his temper in check by only a thin thread. He pointed at the baby in the basket-carrier thing. "He's not."

"And where is he supposed to go?"

"That's not my problem."

She pulled her employment agreement from her pocket. "It might be the agency's mistake that they told me it was okay to bring my son, but this is *your* agreement and I don't recall anywhere in here that says I can't bring a child. If you won't let me keep him, you're in breach…" She paused, smiled. "All you have to do is give me a check for a thousand dollars and I'm out of here."

Jeb was just about to remind her that since the agency made the mistake they were responsible to reimburse the money she spent, until she said the magic words…

"And you can find yourself another housekeeper."

All the wind evaporated from his angry sails. He *couldn't* find himself another housekeeper. Thanks to Maria, the women in town wouldn't work for him and none of the other California candidates he'd interviewed had been suitable. She was the only person he considered qualified. If she left, he started at square one and it would take him months to find someone willing to work for him. He didn't have months. He had potential clients coming to see the ranch in three weeks.

He took a pace back. "Haul your gear inside. I'll send Slim out to show you to your quarters." He turned to leave, but spun to face her again.

"And keep him," he said, pointing at the happy baby, "out of my sight."

He pivoted toward the house and strode to his office, all but hyperventilating from fury. He *couldn't* live with a baby for the entire year of her employment agreement. And if money could get her to leave, he would happily pay it. Just as soon as his potential clients were gone, he'd give her the damned thousand dollars and she could leave.

But that meant he had only three weeks to find a replacement. He fell into the tall-backed chair, grabbed the phone receiver and punched in the number of the employment agency from memory.

"A baby!" he sputtered. His thoughts were so angry he couldn't merely think them; he spoke out loud. "What kind of woman brings a baby to a job?"

"The kind forced to live somewhere for a year."

Seeing Slim standing in the doorway of his office, Jeb slammed the receiver in the phone cradle again. A bear of a man, with shoulders as wide as the doorway, Jim Cavanaugh was one of those people whose childhood nickname no longer fit, but who couldn't seem to get rid of it.

"Don't take her side."

"I'm not taking her side. I'm just stating a fact. The agency told her it was okay for her to bring her child. And since she and the kid are here, what harm can it do to give her a chance?"

What harm? Slim, of all people, should know exactly why he didn't want a baby around. "I'm hiring somebody else."

Slim planted his hands on his hips. "Oh, really? Where do you propose to find someone? Are you going to trust the agency that already got your instructions wrong with Sophie? Or are you going to try the girls in town again?"

Jeb scowled.

"Look, Jeb. I'm not the kind to state the obvious, but you have to keep her."

Jeb picked up a pencil and tapped it on the

mouse pad beside his computer keyboard. "Fine. Whatever. She's got three weeks."

"Just long enough to get the house clean for your clients? You're all heart."

"Don't push it, Slim."

Slim left the room, annoyed that the surfer girl wasn't getting much of a chance to prove herself, but Jeb didn't care. He picked up the phone again. Too much was at stake for him to deviate from his plan. Having a baby around might seem insignificant, but Jeb had seen many a little thing topple big plans. There was no way he'd risk his future—his home—when it had taken him so long to get one.

He'd spent his childhood hopping from one tropical paradise to another with his wealthy jet-setter parents. His first year at university he thought he should feel "settled"—since he was actually staying in one place for nine consecutive months—but he didn't. Eventually he realized "home" was more than a house or a place to consistently lay his head. For the next two years he'd longed for the sense of direction, sense of purpose, sense of identity that the other students had.

Then he had gotten an apartment off

campus, next door to two very determined brothers. Ranchers. People of substance. People with roots and identity. People whose great-great-grandparents had settled in Montana and who knew that a hundred years from now their property would still be Langford land.

With too much money and very little meaning to his life, Jeb wanted so much to be one of them that he'd married their sister Laine, and bought the ranch he now lived on, prepared to fulfill his adopted destiny of handing his ranch down from one generation of Worthingtons to the next… Until he and Laine divorced.

His dream had died a sudden, brutal death, but after only a few weeks of wallowing in misery, it dawned on him that he didn't need to have a wife or kids or even a "person" to hand down his land. He could still leave a legacy. It would simply be in the form of a foundation—a trust that would keep this ranch running exactly as it was right now for a hundred years after his death.

Just as he always did, he persevered. But only because he didn't deviate from the blueprint he created to achieve his goals.

So no. Sophie Penazzi and her baby were not staying. Might as well start the ball rolling now on finding her replacement.

Two seconds after Jeb strode into his house, Sophie had realized her offer to leave if he would pay her for expenses had been a terrible lapse in judgment. Her horror at making such a stupid mistake must have shown on her face because after Slim had taken her to her room, he'd told her to give him a few minutes and he'd straighten out this mess with Jeb.

Standing in the sitting room of the three-room maid's quarters, admiring the hardwood floors, traditional sofa and chair and big screen TV—quarters much nicer than any apartment she could afford—she took a long breath and said a prayer that Slim would be successful. Not only did this job pay enough to wipe out the debt she owed the hospital for Brady's birth, but also she had nowhere else to go. The thousand dollars she'd demanded as compensation for driving to the ranch wouldn't pay the first month's rent on a new apartment; forget about the additional security deposit required on most places. If she lost this job, she and her baby would be dead broke and homeless.

With her little boy asleep in the bedroom, she cursed Brady's dad for dumping them the way he had, putting her in the predicament of having no money and a child to raise. But rather than fall victim to self-pity, she reminded herself that Mick wasn't as much to blame for bailing on them as she was for trusting him. She'd been brought into the world by parents whose careers always came first. She shouldn't have been surprised that when she got pregnant, Mick no longer saw her as a partner, but a burden, maybe even an obstacle to the life he had planned. He'd never hidden his determination to arrange his world just the way he wanted it. She hadn't been blind to his self-centeredness. But she had stupidly believed love could cause him to make room for the new addition to their lives.

She shook her head in wonder. Thinking love would cause him to make room for Brady was just another way of saying that she believed that with enough love Mick would change. After twenty-two years of jumping through hoops for parents who never found a way to have any time for her, she should have known better than to take up with someone as career oriented as Mick. But she hadn't. He had to dump her before she finally got the message. People didn't change. And she wouldn't again make the mistake of believing they could.

A knock sounded on her door, then Slim opened it and poked his head inside. "You're set for a while."

"A while?"

"It sometimes takes Jeb a bit of time to realize everything's going to be okay, but he'll come around. You just do a good job."

Sophie smiled and nodded, but from the guarded expression on Slim's face she knew he hadn't really made any headway with her stubborn boss. Jeb Worthington wasn't happy with her and her baby and though he'd told her to stow her gear that didn't really mean she was staying. She appreciated the ranch foreman going to bat for her, but she wasn't the kind to let somebody else fight her battles. Once Slim disappeared down the hall, she checked to make sure Brady was sleeping soundly, scooped up the baby monitor and went in search of Jeb.

She walked down empty corridors and

through half-furnished rooms confused that a man who seemed to have money didn't surround himself with creature comforts. Eventually she found him in his office. Pacing behind the huge cherrywood desk and tall-back black leather chair, he talked on the phone, his boots clicking on the hardwood floor.

"I'd like to speak with Mrs. Gunther, please." He was so absorbed in his pacing that Sophie knew he hadn't noticed her in his doorway. She let her gaze slide up his jean-clad legs, the lightweight plaid shirt, his broad shoulders. "It's Jeb Worthington."

If his jerky strides were anything to go by, patience wasn't his strong suit… Or maybe he wasn't a man accustomed to sitting or even being inside? The natural tan of his face and hands said he was more at home in the elements than his office. Plus, his body was trimmed, toned, muscled—probably from hard work, not a gym.

Her gaze moved up again, until it reached his face. Straight nose. Silky looking black hair. Her breath stuttered in her chest. Wow. How had she missed that he was gorgeous?

Thinking back on the day she interviewed with him, she winced, remembering that she *had* noticed. In fact, she remembered wanting to swoon when he walked into the room. She'd been so excited about the great pay and benefits he'd offered her that she'd forgotten that.

"Mrs. Gunther?"

He stopped his pacing, turned to the heavy drapes that covered a wall of windows, affording Sophie the opportunity to see his strong back that tapered into a taut waist and trim hips.

"When you sent me a woman with a baby, I think you forgot my housekeeper has to live in."

Jeb's conversation brought her back to the present and reminded her of another complication with her employment at this ranch. She was ready to fight to keep a job that meant she'd have to live with a man who was so attractive she'd wanted to swoon the first time she'd seen him.

Was that smart?

"The ranch is so far out in the country we only go into town for supplies once a month. She can't commute. And it's impractical for her to hire a baby-sitter. That is, if she can even find one. I had to go the whole way to California to find her."

His voice went from businesslike to impatient to downright angry so quickly that Sophie blinked. Maybe she was the one being too hasty? He was a grouch with little to no patience with mistakes. Not even honest ones. Yet instead of running for cover before he saw her eavesdropping, she stood gazing at him like a star-struck teenager, as if how he behaved didn't matter; he was so good-looking that she could forgive his being a little grouchy.

That wasn't like her at all. And it also wasn't right.

"Okay, let's just say we both agree that mistakes happen. I can appreciate that your staff got the instruction wrong. That doesn't change the fact that her having a baby is a deal breaker. I can't keep her."

Sophie's mouth fell open in dismay, but as he paused to listen to Mrs. Gunther, he turned in her direction and she jumped away from the open doorway into the hall, flattening herself against the wall so he wouldn't see her.

"I know that under the circumstances, especially with the flexible schedule, it doesn't seem that a baby would be a problem. But they're a hindrance, a distraction. I can't risk everything I've put into this company because she can't get her work done."

Though her heart had been pounding a hundred beats a second, his argument caused it to settle down and she frowned. *That* was all he was worried about? That she wouldn't get her work done? Was he nuts? Every mother in the world cooked and cleaned while caring for her children. Of course she could get her work done.

"Just start gathering résumés again. Get me somebody who can do everything I need done and this time without a baby."

He slammed the phone receiver into the cradle and Sophie hightailed it out of the corridor. But as she scrambled back to her quarters, she smiled, suddenly inspired. She might not have been able to get her parents or Mick to change, but the problem she had with Jeb Worthington wasn't about getting him to change. It was only about getting him to change his mind. To keep this job, all she had to do was *show* him that she could get her work done even *with* Brady in the room, underfoot, in the baby carrier slung over her back.

Actually that really was the way to go. Rather than tiptoe around Brady, the best thing to do would be to demonstrate that—just like every other mother on the planet—she could get her work done with her baby, not in spite of her baby.

And forget all about the fact that he was good-looking.

CHAPTER TWO

THOUGH Sophie didn't know what time ranchers woke for morning chores—there had been no reason to tell her because breakfast wasn't her responsibility, only supper was—she set her alarm for four-thirty and bounced out of bed when it rang.

Her plan was to make Jeb the breakfast of his dreams and serve it to him with Brady sitting in the high chair only a few feet away. The baby might goo and coo, but who could object to happy baby sounds? No one. Her boss would have good food and good company and he'd see there were more reasons to like having Brady around than reasons to kick them off the ranch.

Piece of cake.

After dressing herself in a T-shirt and blue jeans, she raced to the kitchen taking the baby monitor with her so that she'd hear Brady wake. Then she quickly brewed a pot of coffee, and ran to the refrigerator for fruit. A Tex-Mex omelet would be the main course, but she intended to do this up right and prepare the kind of hearty meal a rancher needed. Fruit cup first. A little oatmeal. Then the omelet, bacon and toast.

Running around the huge kitchen with solid oak cabinets and pale granite counter-tops surrounding the stainless steel appliances, she sliced fruit until five o'clock. Still scurrying, she fried bacon. At five-thirty, she put toast into the stainless steel toaster and by the time six o'clock rolled around she was becoming nervous.

The coffee was stale, the toast cold and the fruit soft. She thought ranchers got up at the crack of dawn? Where the heck was Jeb?

Expecting him to stroll through the door any second, she located everything needed to cook the omelet, which she couldn't actually prepare until he was ready to eat. When all the ingredients sat on the counter by the stainless steel stove, she stopped moving.

Where was he?

Six turned into six-thirty. The sound of Brady waking crackled through the monitor, and she went to the bedroom and quickly got him dressed. Then she came back to the kitchen and slid him into his high chair that she'd already placed at the table. At seven-fifteen, Jeb finally strolled into the kitchen and stopped dead in his tracks when he saw her.

Leaning against the stove, arms crossed on her chest, she narrowed her eyes at him. His dark hair and brooding gray-green eyes could stop the heart of any normal woman, and Sophie had to admit hers stuttered a bit just at the sight of him. But she reminded herself that her need to keep this job trumped any romantic notions. She needed employment, not to be a lovesick puppy over a self-absorbed man.

Jeb almost asked Sophie why she was standing in his kitchen. He liked being alone when he first got up. That's why breakfast wasn't on her list of duties.

Instead he reminded himself he had to be nice so she'd not only stay and clean the house for the clients arriving in three weeks, but also to mend his reputation. When she left, he'd give her the thousand dollars she'd requested so that her only complaint could be that her baby hadn't fit into ranch life. And if she just happened to stop in town on her way back to California, and mention that Jeb had given her a nice bonus, so much the better.

Walking to the counter with the coffee-maker, he said, "Good morning."

"I'm not sure I'd drink that. I made it at four-thirty."

He turned and gaped at her. "Why?"

"Because I thought all ranchers got up early and I was trying to please you."

This time his eyes narrowed. "Trying to please me?"

"Because I'm sorry."

"What the hell do you have to be sorry for? You said the agency told you it was okay to bring your son."

"I should have confirmed that with you."

At the repentant expression on her face, Jeb turned away from her. It wasn't her fault that the agency had got his instructions wrong. Yet, the woman he would fire as soon as his prospective clients had seen the house, had apologized *and* made him breakfast.

A wave of guilt rode through him like a wild stallion. He glanced over, ready to thank her for her trouble but also to tell her that her work was all for nothing because he wasn't a breakfast person. But when he looked at her, the words froze in his mouth. Her dark brown eyes snagged his gaze and he totally forgot the speech he had planned.

"I haven't yet made the omelet and I can make fresh toast," she said, her eyes brightening with hope and her lips teasing upward into a smile. "So, if you're hungry, I can have a hot breakfast for you in no time."

He swallowed. Good grief, she was pretty. But more than that, she was nice. Nice enough that he forgot all about counteracting Maria's claims that he was a grouchy boss. Staring into her dark brown orbs, it didn't matter what anyone else thought. He'd feel like a heel all day if he didn't eat the breakfast she'd planned.

"Sure. I'd love an omelet."

"Great! You sit. I'll put on a fresh pot of coffee."

She made the coffee first, and without another word to him, busied herself breaking eggs into a bowl and adding chopped vegetables from a plate beside the stove.

Taking a seat at the round oak table, Jeb finally noticed the high chair…and her baby.

The little boy with hair pointing to all four corners of the world sat no more than three feet away from him.

The kid grinned toothlessly at him. Jeb sucked in another breath, debating how to remind Sophie that she was supposed to keep her baby out of his way, but within what seemed like seconds she appeared at the table, delicious smelling omelet on one of his everyday dishes.

"I'm really sorry about all this."

The room suddenly felt small and cramped. To his right was a baby. A perfect, healthy, happy child. To his left that little boy's mom. A perfect, healthy, sexy woman.

Lord, he should have kept Maria. She might have been attracted to him, but he hadn't been attracted to her and that situation he could have controlled.

Prepared to eat his omelet in record time and get the hell out of here, he picked up his fork. Much to his horror, Sophie took a seat, putting herself between him and her baby. She lifted a tiny spoon from a small plate of mushy food and directed it to her baby's mouth.

"I wish I had known you didn't want a

woman with a child. I wouldn't even have interviewed."

The kid smacked his lips at the taste of the putrid looking yellowish mush. Jeb forced breath into his lung. "It's not your fault."

The baby clapped his hands together with glee as Sophie got another spoon of the mush and said, "I feel responsible."

Jeb's muscles began to quiver from the effort of not reacting to her or her child and he knew that was stupid, foolish. She was just another woman. His housekeeper. His *employee*. Being attracted to her was wrong in so many ways he couldn't even count them. He tried to convince himself that the spike in his heart rate was from having a baby so near, but he knew the real reason was Sophie herself. She was feeling guilty for things that weren't her fault and injustice always made him want to fight for the underdog. He couldn't fight for the woman he was firing. *He* was the enemy.

"Look, you have to stop taking the blame for everything."

"I can't help it." She laughed. "It's been woven into my DNA."

Her laugh skimmed along his nerve

endings like a spring breeze dances through new grass, but her words worked their way past his hormones and found his brain. He'd never wondered about this single woman's reasons for taking a job at a ranch so far out of town she had to live in, but her last comment was very telling. Though his parents would have happily let him become a beach bum, he'd had plenty of school friends who couldn't quite measure up to family expectations.

He glanced at the baby, and then caught Sophie's gaze again. He couldn't be so crass as to come right out and ask if her parents had frowned on her having a baby without being married. So, he took a shortcut and asked simply, "Crappy parents?"

"Depends on whose perspective you get. My dad's a doctor. Salt of the earth. Wins awards."

"And your mom?"

"University professor. Brilliant. Her students hang on her every word and she lets them hang out in her living room."

"But she doesn't have any room for her daughter?"

"It's more that her daughter never really fit." She fed the baby another spoon of yellow mush then smiled at Jeb. "With either of them. Not the surgeon filled with heart or the university professor everybody loved."

"And you think that's your fault?"

She shrugged. "Yes and no. I mean, logically, I know that my parents have to take responsibility for not making time for their daughter, but I also know we create our own destinies. I'd rather take responsibility than be a whiner."

Her comment was so unexpected that he nearly spit out his coffee on a laugh. And that scared him more than feeling sorry for her. He always was a sucker for a woman who could make him laugh. And this woman had not only gotten him to sit down to breakfast, and talk about her personal life, but now she'd made him laugh. If he didn't straighten things out between them and quickly, she'd have him spilling the story of his life. And that couldn't happen.

He rose from the table. "Okay. Here's how this is going to go down. I don't want you taking the blame for things you didn't do. I don't want you making breakfast. I never eat when I first get up. I just take coffee to the barn with me." He walked to the cupboard, pulled out his travel mug and set it on the counter with the coffeemaker. "I don't want anything special like this from you again. The job description doesn't include breakfast. So don't make it." He poured coffee into his mug. "I want the house clean, my laundry done and supper made. Nothing else."

He strode to the door, grabbed the knob and faced her. "You got that?"

She nodded.

"Good."

But as Jeb was walking to the barn, he wondered if Sophie really did understand what he'd said. It was easy to tell from her few comments about her parents that she'd probably spent her childhood trying to please them, which made her one of those people who was always working to fix everybody around them.

Lord, if she ever found out the truth of his life, she'd have a field day.

He stopped walking. Actually that wasn't funny. In less than a day, she'd already gotten him to sit down to a breakfast he didn't want, withhold a reprimand for not keeping her baby out of his sight *and* engage in a personal discussion about her parents. She'd grown up looking and listening for clues of how her parents felt. If he spent too much time in her company, she'd sense he was hiding something and she might even make it her life's mission to get him to talk about it so she could help him.

He was strong enough—stubborn enough—that he didn't believe he'd spill his guts and tell her things he didn't want anybody to know, but why risk it?

Her primary function was to prepare his house for his clients. He could easily take cooking off her list of duties and never even have to worry that their paths would cross.

That was a much better idea than sitting three feet away from her and her child, risking that she'd work whatever magic she wove and somehow get him talking about himself.

Sophie was in the middle of supper preparations when Jeb opened the back door and strode into the kitchen talking. "Sophie, can you come back to the office with me for a minute?"

She looked up from the pepper she was chopping then glanced at the baby monitor on the counter. Brady had just gone to sleep. She didn't believe he would wake up. She could leave him for five minutes without the monitor…right?

"This won't take long."

She smiled and said, "Sure," but waited until Jeb was in the hall leading to the front foyer, before she snatched the monitor from the counter as she passed it. He hadn't said a word about Brady that morning, but that was actually the problem. She'd never met a person who didn't oohh and ahh over her baby. The fact that her boss hadn't even addressed the adorable child sitting in the high chair next to him could mean he really was one of those people who didn't like babies. If that was the case, she might have to rethink her strategy. Stuffing the monitor into her apron pocket, she followed Jeb into the office.

"Have a seat."

She sat with a smile. A big smile. He wouldn't have called her into his office unless he had something important to discuss. She had to show him that no matter what he wanted she'd do her best to accommodate him. No matter what he said, she would agree.

He sat on the big leather chair behind the desk. "I've decided to modify your duties."

Great! More work! Finally a way to prove

herself! If she had any luck, he'd changed his mind about breakfast. She was a much better cook than housekeeper, and breakfast was her specialty. She could easily impress him with omelets and waffles. If he'd simply add breakfast into her duties, he'd beg her to stay the entire year of their contract.

"I'm taking *all* cooking off your list of responsibilities."

All the breath whooshed out of Sophie's lungs. "What?"

"The cooking. I'm taking it off your list of job duties. You have plenty to do without it."

"No, I don't!"

He fiddled with some papers on his desk, then looked up at her. "Yes, you do." He leaned back in the seat. "You were surprised this morning when I didn't get up with the sun because you thought that's what ranchers do."

Heartsick because she'd lost her best way to impress him, Sophie nodded.

"Usually that's true, but in our case I don't really run the Silver Saddle. I run the ranch management company that owns the Silver Saddle. As ranch foreman, Slim gets up and gets the day going with the hands. That's what every foreman at every ranch my company manages does. I personally don't run the ranches. I have great foremen who do that."

"And what do you do?"

"I market my business." He sat up again, leaning forward on his desk, obviously comfortable talking about his company, looking like a lethal combination of sexy rancher and savvy businessman. "This house," he said, pointing around in a circle, "is a big part of my marketing plan. Remember, during the interview I told you I had frequent guests?"

"Yes."

"The guests are wealthy people who buy ranches so that they have a private country retreat. Somewhere they can go and be themselves. Be comfortable. But after a year or so of owning a ranch, they realize how much trouble it is to run it, so they go looking for somebody like me. Or a company like mine. We do the work for the ranch. They reap the benefits."

"I'm still not sure what this has to do with me."

"If it were just me living here, I wouldn't have a housekeeper. I'd let the dust pile up. But because of my guests I need the place to be clean. Which means you're part of the business. You're not really a maid. You're more of an extension of the ranch management company, making sure everything sparkles for clients." He relaxed and leaned back on his chair again. "So that's all I want you to do."

Knowing he was waiting for a reaction from her, Sophie stalled for time by running her tongue along her lips. A smart woman would simply say okay. Sophie told herself to say okay. To smile. To accept his order. Not to argue that cooking was her forte and if he'd just allow her cook for him, he'd never let her leave.

She took a breath. Told herself again to simply say, "Okay."

Just say okay!

She opened her mouth, but instead of her one-word agreement, she found herself saying, "This is because of Brady, isn't it?" But once the words were out of her mouth, she wasn't sorry. The guy was going to fire her for something that wasn't her fault and she'd be damned if she'd roll over and play dead.

"No."

"Yes. It is." She rose from her seat and leaned across the desk. "You didn't even look at him this morning."

He rose, pressed his hands on his desk and leaned toward her. "I asked you to keep him away from me. If we push everything else aside in this discussion, the bottom line is you disobeyed an order from your boss. Now you're paying the consequences."

"But Brady's a sweet kid!" She paused, drew in a breath. "You know what? Maybe if you'd spend some time with him *you* might get a little sweeter."

He gaped at her. "Are you kidding me? After disobeying a direct order, now you're sassing?"

Sophie reared back and pressed her palm to her mouth. In her zeal to prove that she could work with Brady, she'd *forgotten* that he didn't want the baby in the room. But he was right about the sassing. *That* didn't help her cause at all. And she knew better. But when it came to Brady, her motherly instincts always surprised her.

He sighed. "Look, I have potential clients arriving in three weeks. What I need… No, what the *business* needs is for this big house to be clean, looking like the perfect retreat from the hustle and bustle of a busy life. After that you can leave. I'll even give you the thousand dollars. I just want you and your baby gone."

Tears filled her eyes. *She was being fired because she had a baby.* She shook her head in disbelief. "He doesn't talk. If he makes a sound it's a gurgle of happiness. How could you possibly be opposed to that?"

"It doesn't matter. This is my ranch. My business and my home. I set the rules. I told you I didn't want to see your baby, but you either chose not to keep him out of my way or *couldn't* keep him out of my way as requested. The arrangement failed." He leaned back in his chair again. "Now, you can stay three weeks because I do need the house cleaned for the clients, and I'm even giving you the extra thousand you asked for. But after that you're gone. I won't have a baby here."

CHAPTER THREE

Sophie watched television until eleven that night, hoping to make herself tired. But even after hours of mindless TV her upset over losing her job made her too restless to go to bed.

After checking to make sure Brady was in a deep sleep, she slid into her one-piece bathing suit and the matching terry-cloth cover-up then grabbed the portable baby monitor from the bedside table. Slim had shown her a swimming pool when he gave her the tour of the house and said she was free to use it. Of course, that was before she had been fired, but she didn't care. She was restless and needed to make herself tired. She was having a swim.

She opened the door to her suite slowly, not wanting to run in to anyone since her cover-up was short and she felt uncomfortable walking around only half dressed.

Common sense told her she had no reason to fear. It was late. She was on the first floor. Her boss's suite of rooms was on the second floor. Slim had a cabin behind the homestead. Only a few hands actually slept in the bunkhouse, but even they were so far from the house that no one would see her. She was perfectly safe.

She took a breath, stole down the short hall that led to the kitchen and then slipped into the family room with French doors that led to the pool. In another two steps, she was standing on the stone patio.

Silence descended on her like a warm blanket. The city always had sound. Background noise. A person might grow accustomed to it and not "hear" it, but it was always there. On this ranch, so far away from civilization, she learned the meaning of the word silence.

Removing her cover-up, she glanced around in awe. Except for dim lights illuminating the blue water of the pool, this world was also inky-black. Remembering something about seeing stars in the country, she quickly glanced up and sighed.

"Oh, my gosh."

"Oh, my gosh what?"

On a gasp, Sophie spun around to find Jeb walking out of the shadows behind her. Water flattened his thick black hair and droplets cascaded from his shoulders and down his broad chest, making trails through whorls of dark hair leading to six-pack abs. Wet black swimming trucks clung precariously to lean hips and a butt made for a woman to sink her fingernails into in the throes of passion.

Even as her mouth went dry, she groaned inwardly. How could she be attracted to the man who had just fired her?

"Oh, my gosh what?" He repeated his question as he walked over to her, stopping within arm's reach.

Awareness shimmied through her. With her cover-up in her hand and wearing only her bathing suit, she wasn't quite as naked as he was, but they were both scantily dressed, alone, in the darkness.

She pulled in a breath. This was ridiculous. Not only were they were both sufficiently covered, but also she was furious with him and he clearly didn't like her. There was no reason to remind him of that, but she wouldn't cower from him, either.

She forced herself to meet his gaze. "The stars. There are so many."

"You have big city syndrome," he growled, back to being the grouchy boss. "The sky is always lit over a city, blocking one of nature's greatest gifts. A starry night."

He looked up into the star-spangled darkness and her gaze skimmed his broad chest and perfect tummy. He was, quite literally, the sexiest man she'd ever seen.

"Yeah. We certainly don't have stars like this in the city." She swallowed, desperately trying to will away her attraction. He was a self-centered grouch, who had fired her. He was the last person she wanted to feel anything for. But she couldn't deny that being this close to him, her whole body hummed. She told herself it was just plain foolish to be attracted to a man she didn't even like. Yet, here she stood, her breathing erratic, her nerve endings on red alert.

"I'll go back to my room."

He snatched a huge green towel from a nearby chaise. "No, I'll go. I'm done with my swim. In about ten seconds the patio will be all yours."

A nervous laugh bubbled up from her.

There was no way she'd force him to leave his own swimming pool. No way she'd give him another thing to complain about. "No. That's okay. You stay. I only came out here to get a breath of fresh air."

She watched his gaze move from her face, down her one-piece suit, pausing on the length of leg exposed beneath the high-cut bottom.

"If you only came out for fresh air, then why are you in a swimsuit?"

Her breathing, which had been erratic, stalled in her chest. His voice might have been strong, detached, but the look he'd given her had been long and slow. He'd taken in every square inch of her and lingered on the part of her that usually drew a man—her legs.

She swallowed.

Knowing she had to get herself out of this and quickly, she tried to fall back on humor. "All right. You caught me. I'm guilty as charged. I wanted a quick swim, but I didn't realize you were using the pool or I wouldn't have come out."

He took a step closer. "I didn't picture you as the one-piece suit type. I figured you more for a bikini girl."

Another nervous laugh escaped her. Was it

her imagination, or was he flirting with her? If he made a pass at her, she wasn't sure if she would melt or faint.

Of course, she could be jumping to conclusions. One little comment didn't necessarily mean he was flirting. He could actually be confused by her choice of swimwear.

"Why a bikini?"

"Don't you surf?"

"No."

"Hum. A California girl who doesn't surf. Another myth debunked."

Relief skittered through her. He wasn't flirting but confused by her. She could breathe again. "You think all California girls surf?"

He caught her gaze, his pale eyes soft and serious in the moonlight. "Yes."

Realization of how close they were slid over her. He was a very different man when he wasn't yelling at her. In fact, from the way he was looking at her she'd never guess he had a problem with her at all.

She licked her suddenly dry lips, feeling reactions and emotions that were more instinctive than conscious. Her eyes desperately wanted to move down again, soak in the beauty and masculinity of his chest, and she struggled to keep them locked with his. Her nerve endings sparkled like the stars overhead.

He stepped back, his gaze still locked with hers. "You'd do well to remember that I'm a grouch and check to make sure the pool isn't occupied the next time you want to swim."

Embarrassment poured through her in a rush of heat. So much for him being a different man when he wasn't yelling.

But even if he couldn't rise above their differences, she could. "I'm sorry. Next time I want to swim I'll ask."

"There's no reason to ask. Just remember that I swim every night around ten-thirty and we'll be fine."

Though his words were appropriate, his voice went back to being soft, hypnotic, resurrecting the sprinkle of gooseflesh that covered her body. She peeked at him, confused again. What was going on here?

Before she could say anything, he turned to the French doors and within seconds was gone.

She shook her head. If she didn't desperately need the money she'd get working here for three weeks, she might be tempted to simply pack her bags and go now. But she did need the money. Not for herself, but for her child. Once again, her motherly instincts won out. But as soon as she had her three weeks pay and the extra thousand dollars, she was out of here.

The next morning, Jeb waited until he heard Sophie head upstairs before he walked into a blissfully empty kitchen. He poured himself a cup of the coffee she'd brewed, and with a huge sigh of relief made his way to his office.

Listening to the messages on his answering machine, he rooted through the stacks of paper looking for a pad to jot down a few numbers, but instead found a note of complaint Maria had left about a leaky faucet. At the time she'd lodged it, she'd been shamelessly coming on to him and he hadn't been sure if it was a genuine complaint or a way to get him to her bedroom.

He cursed. He'd never checked this out and now that he had someone using the suite again, he couldn't let it slide. With Sophie upstairs, he knew he could sneak into her rooms and try the faucet without her even knowing there'd been a problem. After the episode at the swimming pool the night before, that was probably for the best. He'd

decided he wasn't even going to be in the
same room with her again, if at all possible.
So it was good he found the note now when
he could check it out.

He left his office and stealthily made his
way to her suite. The door opened to a sitting
room that smelled soft and feminine. Brady's
baby powders and soaps mixed with more
mature scents of something smoky and sexy,
undoubtedly belonging to Brady's mom and
a picture of her in her innocent one-piece
bathing suite popped into his head. He could
almost feel the warmth of the night, hear her
soft voice as she told him about the stars, and
his groin tightened. He didn't know what it
was about that woman that got to him, but she
had something. He thanked his lucky stars
she'd be leaving soon.

On his way to the bathroom, his gaze fell
on a four-foot-by-four-foot square thing that
sat in the corner of the sitting room and he
stopped. Covered in net, with a bumper guard
decorated with childish characters and
images, the thing was obviously a convenient
place for the baby to sit and play while his
mother worked. But he didn't know that for
sure. He didn't know anything about babies.

He glanced around. With no one in the room to see him, he could indulge his curiosity. He walked over to it and ran his fingers along the smooth plastic that formed a soft rim, probably to protect the kid in someway. He stooped down, peering inside at the toys Sophie had left behind. A stuffed bear. A doll made of soft-looking fabric with yarn for hair. Brightly colored balls and rattles. They were curious things, foreign, almost exotic to a man who hadn't spent two minutes with a baby until his housekeeper had brought one to his home.

"Oh, I'm sorry!"

At the sound of Sophie's voice, his heart all but pounded out of his chest. But with the ease that comes with years of practice, he glanced over indolently, as if she were the one in the wrong.

She stood in the doorway, wild-haired baby on her arm. Her eyes shone brightly with fear, and her breath stuttered into her chest. She should have been angry that he was in her quarters without her permission or even her knowledge. Instead she shook with fear over being in his presence—with her baby. The baby who belonged in this room more than he did.

The guilt he'd felt when she made him breakfast reared its ugly head again. He didn't have a qualm about firing someone for not doing her job; but he wasn't firing Sophie for not doing her job. He was firing her for having a baby.

The little boy cooed, drawing Jeb's gaze to the smiling imp and he swallowed. Did a man ever get over a life blow like the one he had received? Would he ever be able to look at a child without feeling the horrible emptiness?

It didn't matter. His only concern right now was getting himself out of this room before "the fixer" realized something was wrong and asked another one of her damned questions.

He pulled himself up from his crouched position. "My last housekeeper said the bathroom faucet leaks. Does it?"

"I…" She cleared her throat. "I never noticed it leaking."

He strode to the door. "That's what I figured."

He left without another word. Walking down the hall, he tried to focus on being furious with Maria for making his life miserable, but his mind wandered back to soft blankets, sweet smelling toys and blue eyes filled with life and wonder.

He might feel guilty over firing Sophie, but there was no way around it. If the house were clean, he'd give her the three weeks' pay and bonus today just to save his sanity.

CHAPTER FOUR

RIDING the fence line the next day on Jezebel, with Slim beside him on his black stallion, Thunder, Jeb knew he should be enjoying the easy camaraderie with his foreman. The sun was hot and a breeze shimmied through the wildflowers in the shiny green grass. Typically this was when Jeb's focus was its sharpest. Instead the easy pace of the ride lulled him, and his mind wandered back to the sweet smells in Sophie's suite, then to Sophie herself.

She'd been at the ranch three days and every one of those days he'd done something wrong. He knew that the curiosity he felt looking at Brady's toys was an aberration that would leave as soon as the baby did. He also wasn't worried about the conclusions Sophie might have drawn seeing him staring at her baby's things. She'd been so surprised to find him in her suite that he doubted she'd had time to really think about what she'd seen.

But the way his barriers had fallen at the swimming pool couldn't be dismissed so easily. He was her boss, yet he couldn't help asking why she didn't wear a bikini. He couldn't stop himself from looking at her legs. He couldn't keep his voice level, disciplined, authoritative. So he'd planned to simply avoid her, but that hadn't worked out, either. After their contact in her suite, he had to admit he was considering working in the barn and even staying out of the kitchen except to get coffee.

He shook his head in disgust. He hated being out of control. Shouldn't he be able to handle this better?

Of course he should! So what if she was attractive? He was an enormously successful businessman, whose big, bad ranch foremen all but shivered in their boots when they had meetings with him. How could one five-foot-six California girl cause him to forget everything he knew about keeping employees in line?

They were almost back at the barn when Jeb came out of his thoughts and asked Slim about the trouble they'd been having with hikers walking the ranch trails.

"Did you hear anything I said?"

"I heard everything you said."

"Then you'd know I already told you I met with the guy who seems to be organizing the hikes and told him it was no problem for him to bring people on the ranch as long as they stayed in the back of the property, away from the cattle and picked up after themselves."

As Slim said that, Sophie came around the corner of the barn. "Hey!"

"Hey!" Slim called, waving to her. "How's Brady?"

Jeb glanced over at him. He knew the kid's name?

"He's fine. We're both great." She turned and displayed a backpack-like baby carrier in which Brady sat, chewing on a thick plastic ring. "We're going for a walk."

Slim nodded and smiled and Jeb took advantage of everybody's preoccupation with chitchat to peek at the length of leg exposed beneath her jean shorts. Today her thick hair was caught up in a bouncy ponytail and she wore a fancy top with seashells or something dangling from the U-shaped neckline, but as always Jeb's attention was caught by her legs. They were perfect.

"Oh, don't mind him. I don't know where the hell his mind's been all morning." Slim poked him in the arm. "Are you in there, Jeb?"

Jeb's heart froze in his chest. He hoped to hell they simply thought he'd been wool-gathering and no one had caught him staring at Sophie's legs, but one look at Slim's sly expression and he knew his foreman had caught every second of it.

Shading her eyes from the sun with her right hand, Sophie smiled up at him as Jezebel began to do a two-step, once again picking up on his nervousness around his housekeeper and her baby.

"I asked if you minded if Brady and I explore."

"No. I don't mind if you take a walk." He tugged on his horse's reins, directing Jezebel toward the barn. "But you're not familiar enough with the ranch to explore. Stay on the dirt roads."

Sophie nodded and walked off. Jeb watched Slim's gaze follow her, before he yanked on the stallion's reins and turned him in the direction to catch up with Jeb. "Well, I'll be damned."

"Probably for the sins you've committed," Jeb agreed.

"You like her."

Jeb stopped his horse. "No. I just think she's got great legs."

"And a pretty face and a sweet personality—"

"And a baby."

Slim laughed. "You can fool most people with that gruff voice and apparent hatred of kids, but you forget I know things about you that most people don't know."

Jeb headed for the barn again. "Whatever."

Slim laughed again. "Don't whatever me. Especially when I think it's a damned good sign that you like this girl."

"Right. And you think the fact that she has a baby makes her perfect for me."

Slim grinned. "And from the fact that you brought it up first, I'm guessing you've already thought of it, too."

He hadn't. Not until that very second. But as Slim pointed out it was a "sign" of sorts that the thought had even popped into his head. But where Slim saw it as a good sign, Jeb only felt stupid. Desperate. He hated both.

He looked Slim in the eye. "I keep you

around because you're good at your job. But even you don't get to poke into my personal life. Let this alone or Sophie won't be the only one going in three weeks."

With the dusting and window washing done and nothing else to do, Sophie cleaned the kitchen after lunch the next day.

"What are we going to do once this kitchen is cleaned, Brady?" she asked the baby who sat in the high chair, chewing a teething ring, watching his mom with his big blue eyes. "The man doesn't even have furniture in most of the rooms. Once I dusted the woodwork and windowsills and ran a dry mop over the hardwood floors, I was done.

"Our top priority is keeping you out of his way, but even when we tried to go for a walk we ran into him."

Stacking her few lunch dishes in the dishwasher, she sighed. "I always thought being an efficient housekeeper was the one good thing that came from being left with maids, but in this case I'm sort of working myself out of a job. Julianna would love the irony of this."

She smiled remembering her parents' first

maid, who'd not only taught her to clean, but she'd also taught her to cook. Miss Julie—as she liked to be called—had explained that moms taught daughters to cook, not just to feed their families, but as a way to bond.

Sophie had bonded with Julianna and Julianna had taught her everything she knew, not just about cooking but also about housekeeping.

When Julianna had retired, Florence had also been happy to teach Sophie even more about housekeeping. She'd depended upon Sophie so much that Sophie had felt like she was the maid and Florence was the lady of the house. Luckily she only lasted three months before Sophie's parents discovered what was going on and, horrified, had hired someone a tad more willing to do the work herself rather than "share" it with Sophie.

Laughing, Sophie remembered how mortified her parents had been that Sophie had been housecleaning with the help.

But they didn't realize how that had worked in her favor. In spite of the fact that she didn't have either of her parents' genius IQ, she now had a marketable skill. She could cook and clean well enough to be anybody's housekeeper. It might not please her high-brow parents, but it did pay the bills.

Thinking of her parents made her incredibly sad. Not just for herself but also because they didn't understand what *they* were missing. She loved Brady so much that she would have given up anything for him. Yet her parents didn't have any more time for their grandchild than they'd had for their daughter.

But she and Brady had each other. For the first time in her life she had someone who loved her and she wasn't shortchanging him of the love a child deserved. She'd move heaven and earth to show him he was loved. Wanted. Which was exactly why she wouldn't stay with grouchy Jeb Worthington any longer than she had to to earn the money she needed to get back on her feet. She wouldn't neglect Brady the way her parents had neglected her. She might have to keep herself and Brady off Jeb's radar, but she wasn't hiding him for anybody.

She finished cleaning the kitchen, talking baby talk with Brady and when everything was tidy, she scooped him out of the high chair and carried him through the nearly empty formal dining room and into a hall, which passed two other empty rooms.

What was with this house? Why had Jeb left it so empty? Why would someone as rich as he was not buy furniture?

Looking around as she walked, she decided a busy guy like Jeb might not have had had time to choose sofas and chairs, end tables and lamps, and he most certainly wouldn't know how to "decorate." Not like Paul, the one and only male housekeeper her parents had hired. If Paul ever saw this house, Sophie didn't know if he'd die from the trauma of the neglect he'd perceive or if he'd be in hog heaven. Paul would probably convince Jeb to let him furnish and decorate every empty room—

She stopped. "Oh, my goodness, Brady! I think I just found the way to keep us out from under the boss's feet!"

The next morning when Jeb walked into the kitchen, Sophie was waiting for him. Wearing jean shorts and a tank top, with her dark hair piled on her head in a haphazard way that was somehow sexier than all get out, she stood in front of the kitchen sink, her eyes bright with enthusiasm.

His first instinct was to ignore her. But a fire of indignation ignited in his belly. This was his home, yet he couldn't eat or cook in his own kitchen. Couldn't go for his nightly swim without checking over his shoulder to see if she was sneaking out to join him. And now he couldn't get coffee?

No. Hell no! He was not losing his morning coffee!

He walked to the counter, reached into the cupboard for his travel mug and pulled it down. On his way to the coffeepot he'd noticed the high chair was empty. She was doing as he'd asked. Keeping the baby out of his sight.

"Where were you all day yesterday?"

She broke the silence with her question, but Jeb looked away, pretending great interest in putting cream in his coffee.

"I searched everywhere but I totally missed you. You're a hard man to find."

"Not really. I've got a company to run. This ranch is part of it."

"Unless I misinterpreted you, you also have a house that needs fixing before your guests arrive."

"It doesn't need fixing...it needs to be cleaned."

"Well, see, that's where you and I differ." She motioned to the table, indicating they should sit but he didn't budge from the counter. "Come on, this will only take a minute."

"Slim and I are flying to Wyoming today to look at the ranch of another potential client. We can't be late."

"I'll talk fast."

"Fine."

She pulled in a breath. He kept his eyes on her face, knowing damned well that her breasts had risen and fallen, but he wasn't allowed to look. Wouldn't look. *Refused* to look.

"I've noticed that your house is barely furnished."

He brought his coffee to his mouth and peered at her over the rim of the mug. "Because I don't want prospective clients to see my furniture. I want them to see the place empty enough to envision their furniture in the rooms."

"Good point. Except these ranches you manage are second homes for your clients. They won't be moving their furniture to a ranch they bought as a second home. And when they come here to check out your ranch, they may be looking for inspiration."

Confused, he scrunched up his face and said, "What the hell are you talking about?"

"I think you mixed up real estate concepts. If you're selling a house, it is true that you want everything to be neutral so buyers will see their own things when they walk through the rooms. But you're not selling this house. You're selling the idea that the second home of a ranch is cozy and comfy and private. You're selling privacy."

"I think the secluded nature of most ranches accomplishes that."

"Yes, but not the comfort part."

He was losing the battle to keep his eyes on her face, mostly because she was pretty enough that gazing at her face also resurrected a few thousand male fantasies. Knowing he had to get the hell out of here, he glanced at his watch. "What's your point?"

"That most women would come into this house and not be comfortable. If you're trying to create a mood, and I think you are, your house needs to be decorated."

"Oh, no. No decorator! No fancy sofas, sea of knickknacks and glass tables that can be broken."

She laughed. "Agreed. When I pick some new things for this house, I'll be going on the same principles you've already established. Comfort. Peace. Privacy."

His eyes narrowed. "When *you* pick some new things?"

"Yes." She pulled in a breath. "Okay, look. You already know I need the money or I wouldn't be here. I'm going to be really honest with you and admit that I could probably get this house clean by the end of the week. But if I clean everything this week and leave, by the time your clients get here in three weeks, it'll be dusty again."

He frowned. "What you're really saying is you'd like something to do in between dustings?"

"Yes."

He didn't cotton to boredom himself, but her idea of how to fill her time wasn't practical. "Even if I agreed with you about the house needing a little more furniture, how are you going to shop? Town is forty miles from here and once you get there you won't find a big selection of furniture or anything beyond household necessities."

"Ever heard of the Internet? I can buy anything you need and have it delivered to your front door."

He gaped at her. "I'm supposed to give you a credit card?"

"Nope. All you have to do is set up an online account that has limited uses and limited access. You can give me a budget. You can check my purchases every day." She paused and smiled. "Unfortunately it will mean I'll have to use your computer."

That stopped him. If she stayed in one place for several hours a day, avoiding her would be abundantly easier. "You'll be using my office?"

She grimaced. "Sorry. I don't have a laptop."

"But you'd be in the office all day?"

"Not all day, but a good bit of the day."

"How many hours?"

"I'm not sure."

"But several?"

She grimaced again and nodded.

For several hours a day, every day, she'd be out of his hair? He could use his kitchen. Make a sandwich with cold cuts instead of grilling a burger for lunch. Have a salad.

He picked up his mug. "Sounds like a good idea. You go cruising online today, looking for things you like and I'll set up an account tomorrow."

"Just like that?"

He nodded. "Just like that."

"You aren't going to tell me what you like?"

"You're supposed to be decorating for a woman. I'm not a woman. I just want the place to be comfortable. And not foo-foo. And no pink."

"What's my budget?"

Halfway to the door he paused, faced her. "Let me think about that a bit. Try to come up with a ballpark figure on big ticket items so I have an idea of the least amount of money you'll need, and then I'll give you a number."

Closing the kitchen door behind himself, Jeb smiled. They'd done it— Well, she'd done it. She'd come up with a way to stay out of his hair for the three weeks he was forced to keep her. He didn't care if it cost him half a million dollars. But there was no way he'd let her know that. All he wanted was for her to be busy and out of his way.

Problem solved.

After Brady awakened from his morning nap the next day, Sophie dressed him in clean clothes and headed out for her first day as a decorator. She was glad it had been easy to convince Jeb to let her furnish his home, but walking through the downstairs, seeing just how empty the house was, she worried that she'd bitten off more than she could chew.

A semiempty house might provide the opportunity to keep herself and Brady out of his hair, but it gave her no clue as to Jeb's taste in furniture, what he would like, or even what he disliked.

Brady on her arm, she roamed from room to room, becoming more and more overwhelmed. The house wasn't merely empty, with virtually no clue of how to fill it, but also it was huge.

Her parents were well-off but this guy was *rich*. Handsome, sexy, grouchy and *rich*.

What the heck made her think she could please him? A man who could afford this house on a piece of property this big could have anything he wanted; and people who could have anything they wanted could be as hard to please as they wanted. What if he'd put off furnishing the place not because he didn't want furniture and not because he didn't have time to do it himself, but because he was so picky nothing appealed to him?

Volunteering to decorate was absolutely the stupidest idea she'd had in a long time.

Finding a stairway off a hidden corridor,

she made her way to the lowest level only to discover another entire floor of rooms. Seeing hardwood floors, a huge white sectional sofa, mahogany bar and a fireplace as she descended the stairway, she assumed the space had been designed to be a family room. Further back she found two suites that she speculated should be guest areas if only because each had its own bath, but on the other side of the family room was a media room—at least partially furnished with a big screen TV and a row of comfortable lounge chairs. Beside that was a gym.

She stepped into the gym and smiled wryly at the weight benches, treadmills, stair climbers and every type of exercise equipment she could think of. Now that she knew Jeb didn't do much ranch work, she wasn't surprised to find a room like this. This was definitely how a man got a great body like the one her boss had.

She ran her fingers along the bars on the sides of two treadmills, wondering why he had two of everything. Did he exercise with a buddy? Did Slim join him?

Even as she thought the last, she opened a door off to the side, thinking it was a closet, and instead discovered a dressing room and beyond that a shower and tub with jets. He had absolutely everything a person would need, but none of the little touches that made a house or any one of the rooms personal—not even a splash of color in paint.

She returned to the dressing room and, looking around, found the closet, filled with fat white towels, soaps and other necessities. Everything was so white it gave her no clue as to her boss's taste. She was just about to close the door when a bit of color caught her eye on the bottom shelf. She stooped down and came face-to-face with a box. Sliding it forward so she could peek inside, she saw nothing but pink. Pink towels, a pink terry-cloth robe, pretty pink hairbrush, even pink weights.

She laughed, thinking it looked like a box of Pepto-Bismol, but her laughter gave way to an unexpected understanding. This gear was for a woman. The second treadmill and stair climber and weight bench were for a female friend.

Oh boy. He had a girlfriend. As if there wasn't enough pressure on her to do a good job, now there was a woman in the picture. Someone else who would judge her taste.

What she didn't expect was the rush of disappointment that followed this discovery. Telling herself it was ridiculous to be disappointed her boss—her *grouchy boss*—had a girlfriend, she shoved the box back into place and wound her way through the hollow-sounding empty room that led to the steps and the first floor.

In the office, she set Brady in the playpen she'd brought in the day before and walked to the desk. Pulling his tall-back leather chair away from the desk to sit, she suddenly felt like an interloper. The rest of the house was so empty it was possible to look around and not discover anything, but this was his domain.

A chunky chocolate-colored leather sofa and chair created a seating area atop a Native American print rug that protected the hardwood floor. From the papers strewn over the rough-hewn wood sofa table in the center of the grouping, she guessed that was where Jeb and Slim created the proposals for clients.

A bookcase took up the entire wall to the left of the desk. She glanced at a few titles, mostly mysteries and thrillers. Nothing that give her a clue of how to furnish his huge house.

She pulled open the top desk drawer, looking for a legal pad to make notes and sketch designs. She found nothing but file folders arranged in a long row. With a sigh she began to close the drawer but the name on a tab caught her eye. *Samuel's House.*

If this file contained pictures of the house of a friend—especially a rancher friend—she'd at least get an idea of how his friends lived and know if she was going in the right direction.

She eagerly lifted the file folder from the drawer and opened it on the desktop. To her dismay there were no pictures. Only correspondence.

Dear Mr. Worthington…

On behalf of the staff and children of Samuel's House, we'd like to thank you and your parents for your recent generous donations…

Donations? Samuel's House was a charity? She told herself to close the file, but curiosity got the better of her and she flipped the first letter over and found a second.

Dear Mr. Worthington…
Thank you again for remembering
Samuel's House with your recent gener-
ous donation.

After the third letter, her mouth had
dropped in awe. Samuel's House was obviously a home for children. She glanced down
at the other file folders and quickly scanned
the identity tabs, but found no other charities.
She flipped the next page of correspondence in the Samuel's House file.

Dear Mr. Worthington…
Words can't express our gratitude for
your commitment to build a new facility for the children at Samuel's House.

Sophie's eyes popped. He was building an
entire facility?

The generosity exhibited by you and
your parents touches us deeply. The children who come to us are as much in need
of emotional help as they are basic necessities of life. The new buildings to be
erected by your family will provide us

with opportunities to instill confidence in our children, even as they learn good sportsmanship and get much needed physical activity.

We hope you'll visit us again soon. The children always enjoy seeing you.

Closing the file, Sophie tried to catch her breath. If she'd thought he was rich before this, her eyes had been opened even wider. The man could afford to build an entire facility for what appeared to be an orphanage.

But his money took a back seat to an even bigger realization. Grouchy Jeb Worthington, the man who supposedly hated kids, supported an orphanage. She leaned back on the chair. That didn't make any sense at all.

CHAPTER FIVE

JEB ambled into the empty kitchen, smiling to himself. With Sophie busy elsewhere in the house, he no longer had to avoid her. Their paths legitimately didn't cross.

He laughed as he made a sandwich to take back to the barn office. He could be very clever when he needed to be. Now it didn't matter that his hormones went crazy when they were in the same room. They'd never be in the same room.

He finished his sandwich and headed out again, but at the kitchen door he realized he needed a file from his desk. He pivoted and marched to his office and found Sophie already in his desk chair.

All right. Fine. So his plan wasn't as good at keeping them apart as he'd thought. But this would be a simple encounter. A minute tops. Nothing to worry about.

"Don't get up," he said, talking as he walked in. But the scent of something heavenly sweet—like roses or peaches—instantly engulfed him. He didn't know what brand of soap or shampoo she used, but it filled the air with a scent so feminine it instantly transmitted a message straight to his groin.

Great.

Brady cooed and Jeb glanced in the corner. The baby sat in the playpen Jeb had seen in her suite, chewing on the ear of a stuffed bear. This time his chest contracted. It was as if all the things that made a woman ultrafeminine had gathered in this one space and decided to torment him.

At the desk, he bent and reached for the handle to open the drawer. On its own volition, his gaze drifted to the right, taking in the smooth length of thigh partially hidden beneath his desk, as her scent swirled around him.

This is ridiculous!

His logical side immediately took control, but his masculinity instantly disagreed. Why was it ridiculous to be attracted to a beautiful woman?

Because nothing can come of it.

He grimaced. Unfortunately his logical side was correct.

He turned his attention to sliding open the drawer and reached for the two files he needed—applications of potential clients. But Sophie shifted on the chair, her elbow bumped his shoulder and their gazes met.

Her eyes were dark, smoky, sexy. Her complexion smooth, perfect. Her lips plump, kissable.

His heart speeded up, scrambling his pulse. His gaze locked with hers. He told himself to pull away and get the hell out of this room, but he didn't move. Didn't speak. Barely breathed. Not because she was so pretty, or even because she was suddenly so close. But because she had the same look of confusion on her face that he was sure was on his.

She was attracted to him, too. Though he'd suspected that from their encounter at the swimming pool, he hadn't realized the intensity of what she'd felt. Now he knew she was as powerfully attracted to him as he was to her.

Male confidence filled him. The kind that nudges a boy to ask his first crush to dance. The kind that inspires an adolescent to sweet-talk his first date into a real kiss. The kind that leads a man to seduce his first lover. With one smooth movement he would be close enough to kiss her and he didn't think she'd back away—

Her baby yelped and Jeb jumped as if someone had exploded a firecracker. He grabbed his files and headed for the door without a word. What could he say? *I damned near made the biggest mistake of my life and kissed you? An employee? A woman with a baby?* He couldn't himself believe he'd almost kissed her. How would he explain it to the woman who looked as confused by the attraction as he was?

When he was out of sight, Sophie sucked in a breath and fell back on the chair. He— she— he…

She squeezed her eyes shut then popped them open again. As crazy as it sounded, that man was attracted to her. She'd seen the spark of it in his eyes, felt the electricity of it arching between them. The man who had more money than Sophie could even imagine—enough money to support an orphanage—and was so handsome he made her heart stop… He *liked* her.

Her. Simple, sometimes silly, her.

Even as she realized it didn't make any sense, her heart soared. But Brady screeched again and she shook her head to clear the haze. He might be attracted to her and she might be attracted to him, but he didn't like kids. Support of an orphanage notwithstanding, she'd seen how angry he got around Brady. How standoffish. For Pete's sake, he was firing her because she had the audacity to bring her baby to his ranch.

They could be as hot as Cleopatra and Mark Anthony and absolutely nothing would come of it. She shouldn't even *want* to be attracted to him.

She *didn't* want to be attracted to him.

"I'm sorry, buddy." She rose from the chair and ran to the playpen. "Your mom is here. She isn't going anywhere."

Two days later, having not seen Jeb even once since the episode at his desk, Sophie headed for the barn office. She had waited until he'd been alone for an hour and Brady had been sound asleep for ten minutes, before she took a deep breath for courage and walked the thin sidewalk leading to the barn.

She understood why he was avoiding her,

but she'd come to terms with being attracted to him and wasn't going to let it stand in the way of her doing the best job she could. The truth was he was firing her, and that wouldn't look good on a résumé. She could state that she left his employ because the job was live-in and she had a baby and the ranch had no accommodation for Brady. That would probably even work. But it would work better if Jeb would give her a letter of recommendation.

The only way to get a recommendation would be to do a good job. And the best way to assure that was by getting his approval before she actually made any purchases.

Clutching her yellow legal pad, she followed the sidewalk around the neat-as-a-pin white barn to the back, where Slim had told her she would find the office. She knocked on the frame of the open door before she stepped inside.

"Got a minute?"

He glanced up from his work, his eyes dark and serious. "Not really."

She took a timid step into the room. "This won't take long. I don't feel right spending this kind of money without going over the list of purchases with you first. I don't want to accidentally order thousands of dollars of things you hate."

"We'd just send them back."

"I know, but work with me on this. It would be so much simpler if you'd just take a quick look and tell me I'm going in the right direction."

He sighed and dropped his pencil. "Let me see what you have."

With the trepidation of a schoolgirl about to show her artistry to her favorite teacher, she handed the legal pad across the desk. With the menacing scowl of the lord of darkness, he flipped it open.

She'd cut out prints of furniture, lamps and accessories that she'd made from the pictures she'd found on the Internet and pasted them onto the sheets in the legal pad, creating the groupings she intended in each room.

He flipped from page to page, examining the things she'd chosen. His expression went from grouchy to curious to happy in four flips.

He looked up at her. "These are great."

She winced. "The cutouts leave a lot to be desired."

"No. They're fine. I can see exactly what you intend to do." He glanced down again.

"How did you get pictures of the furniture I already have?"

"I found the Web sites for the brand names and there they were."

"This is all good."

"Really?"

He peered up again, the curious expression back on his face. "Why would you think they weren't?" Before she could answer he shook his head. "Your parents, right?"

She grimaced. "Yes and no. I'd love to blame them for absolutely everything wrong in my life, but the truth is I'm not a decorator."

He flipped back and reviewed the pages he'd already examined. "You may not be a trained decorator but these are really, really good." He caught her gaze again. "I think the fact that you aren't a pro works in your favor. I don't want too polished of a look. I don't want things to be too perfect. These rooms are just the simple rooms of a normal house."

She finally took a seat. "I hope they aren't too simple."

He laughed, turning to the next page. "Maybe what I should have said was that they looked comfortable."

"And not as much as a pink pillow among them."

He worked his way through the sheets in the legal pad again and with every flip of a page, confidence spread through Sophie. This grouchy guy, who to this point seemed unpleaseable, genuinely liked her plans for his home.

After studying the final page, he closed the tablet and handed it across his desk. "Do it."

The joy of accomplishment swelled her heart until it was so big she could barely breathe. "Really? Everything?"

"Everything. I didn't see anything that made me want to run for cover. Every room looks comfortable and homey. Just what I want."

The joy that had swelled her heart gave way to another, more elemental feeling. Connection. She'd finally done something that he more than liked. She'd finally pleased him.

But the brush of their hands as he handed the legal pad to her reminded her that his real problem with her had little to do with her work. They were powerfully attracted to each other. Sexily, steamily attracted to each other. And after the episode in his office, they both knew it.

She pulled in a breath, caught his gaze, forced him to look at her, deal with her, as an employee. Not a woman.

"I really appreciate your confidence in me. I won't disappoint you."

"No," he said slowly, holding her gaze, obviously getting the subliminal message she so desperately wanted to send. "I don't think you will."

"Thank you. I can start pulling this all together tomorrow morning."

"And don't skimp on shipping. I want as much of this done as possible for the client visit. If it means we pay extra to get things here, then that's what we do. Money is no object."

"Okay."

She turned and began to walk out of the room, but he called her back. "Hey, Sophie?"

She swallowed, worried that something negative had occurred to him, so when she faced him again she made sure her expression displayed nothing but confidence. "Yes?"

"Are you going to need any help?"

"Help?"

"You know. Lifting furniture, painting, that kind of thing?"

She hadn't thought of that. Though she

worried it might count as a strike against her, she chose to go with the truth. "Probably."

He glanced down at his work again. "When you need someone, talk to Slim. He'll know who he can spare for a few days or a few hours."

Success tumbled through her. He was treating her totally like an employee. "Thanks."

"You're welcome." He didn't look up. She didn't take offense, but scurrying up the sidewalk to the house, her flip-flops slapping her heels as she ran, a realization occurred to her. He'd treated her well because she'd behaved ultraprofessionally. Proud of her work, she'd let it speak for itself and when he asked a question, she was ready. Her flip-flops again slapped her heels as she made her way through the foyer, and she stopped dead in her tracks. As usual, she wore shorts, a tank top and flip-flops because they were easy to work in, but they really weren't very professional. Which was probably why he didn't see her as an employee first, but a woman. Maybe if she dressed a little more professionally she could add another layer of protection for him?

* * *

With Jeb's permission, Sophie began her shopping spree. For days, she searched the Internet making comparisons, looking for bargains. Though Jeb had told her money was no object, she knew a budget was coming and she didn't want to waste her resources. Slim asked her when she would need assistance from his hands and she said she'd need his guys the next day. That was when the furniture would begin arriving.

"That's cutting it mighty close," he'd said, eating a dish of apple cobbler while Jeb was on the phone schmoozing a potential client. "So, I'm scheduling myself in your team, too."

That surprised her. "Really?"

"Sure. I want to see you succeed." He smiled sheepishly. "You remind me of my oldest daughter."

"You have a family?"

Slim rolled his eyes. "No. They found me under a rock."

She laughed. "I didn't mean that! I'm talking about being married. I didn't even know you had been."

"Was. Like Jeb, I'm a victim of divorce."

He took a bite, chewed and swallowed. "Ranch life isn't easy on a marriage."

Sophie held back an "Oh," of understanding that lifted her spirits. If Jeb had been married to the woman who had owned the pink weights, pink robe and pink everything she'd found in the workout room that meant they didn't belong to a girlfriend. Of course, jumping to the conclusion that those things belonged to an ex-wife might actually be wishful thinking, if only because that meant he was free.

Still, it wouldn't do her any good that he was free. She wouldn't pursue him and he wouldn't pursue her. He didn't like kids and she had one. Plus, she'd be gone in two weeks. No worry about them connecting in any way but professionally.

But she was curious.

And she couldn't ask Slim. If there was one thing she'd seen about ranch life, it was that the people who worked here were loyal. She'd never ask Slim a question he'd have to refuse to answer because she sure as heck knew he'd never betray Jeb.

"So what did you do in California?"

"Do?"

"I thought I'd start sneakily asking you questions about your life and what you like and don't like so I could figure out a gift to buy you as a way to thank you for the pie."

She laughed. It was cobbler, but she didn't correct him. His groans of appreciation while he ate kept her confidence high. "You don't have to buy me a gift."

"I know I don't have to. I want to."

She shook her head. "Just having you appreciate my cooking is thanks enough."

"Since you don't want a gift. How about a ride? Maybe you'd like to take one of the horses out for a few hours."

Her eyes widened. She'd never ridden a horse, but being at this breathtaking ranch had awakened that desire in her. "I'd love to see more of the ranch."

Jeb knew Slim was up to something the second he walked into the kitchen.

"I was just telling Sophie we have a new mare, perfect for someone like her to ride."

He faced her. As had now become the norm, her thick dark hair was swept to the top of her head and pinned out of her way, but tendrils escaped to frame her face. Her bright eyes were shining. Her smile made him want to smile back at her. Which was a really great reason to stop looking at her, but he couldn't very well stare at the coffeepot while talking to her.

"You've never ridden?"

"No."

Her excited expression was almost too much for him to bear and he couldn't stop the chuckle that escaped. "And you want to go riding this afternoon?"

"I've got all the furniture and fixtures ordered. Now I have nothing to do but wait until everything arrives."

"Okay. Great. Whatever."

Slim smiled down at the dish of pastry in front of him. "That's exactly what I told her you'd say. I also told her she couldn't ride alone on her first time. She'd need a guide."

"Right again."

"Which is why I told her I'd watch her baby."

Jeb frowned. "How can you watch the baby when you're going with her?"

"Well, I could go with her but then you'd have to watch Brady."

Jeb's breath caught. He pictured himself... alone...with the little boy with the wild hair and the bright eyes and the smile that could lift the spirits of a man on death row. Terror filled him. He'd never even held a child. He most certainly didn't know how to care for one for several hours.

What if he cried and Jeb couldn't get him to stop?

What if he—required a diaper change?

What if he choked?

"I can't do either."

"You have to do one," Slim pointed out, his smile sly and victorious.

Slim was baiting him! He wanted Jeb to backhandedly admit he had the hots for his new housekeeper by refusing to be alone with her. Or in the alternative, he wanted Jeb to actually go on the ride and spend some time alone with the woman who could make him want to ravish her just being in the same room, hoping something would happen between them. Either way he was meddling, which Jeb had specifically warned him not to.

Jeb took a breath. Slim knew Jeb would never fire him. Their bond went beyond a little teasing about a woman. So he was being clever, but Jeb could be pretty crafty himself. He decided to do exactly what Slim wanted him to do. Go with Sophie. But not with the result Slim expected. His foreman might think he was matchmaking, but Jeb had will-power enough to resist her. He would return without stars in his eyes or lipstick on his mouth because he would make this ride as innocent as possible. He'd shown new employees around the ranch before. And Sophie appeared to like behaving like an employee. So if he treated her solely as an employee when they were alone, in a fairly romantic environment, this ride could actually purge their attraction once and for all.

"Fine. I'll ride with her."

CHAPTER SIX

WHILE Jeb got the horses, Sophie changed into jeans and sensible shoes. She eagerly raced to the barn, ready for the adventure of riding a horse and finally seeing more of the ranch than what was within walking distance.

But, she also had another reason for wanting to take a ride alone with Jeb. It was the perfect opportunity to reinforce that he had nothing to fear from their attraction. She'd already set a tone of professional behavior. This would show him that even in a relaxed setting they could interact like mature adults.

When she reached the barn Jeb stood by two saddled horses. One she recognized as the horse he'd been on the day she arrived at the ranch. The other was a brown mare, a lot less commanding than Jeb's sleek bay.

"Well, let's get going."

After leading the two horses outside, Jeb pointed at the stirrup. "Put your left foot in there, then hoist yourself up, toss your leg over the horse's back and settle yourself in the groove of the saddle."

That sounded simple enough. "Okay." She nodded and slid her foot into the stirrup. But in spite of a decade of aerobics, she couldn't quite hoist herself up and over the broad back of the horse. Not even after three tries.

With a sigh, Jeb put his hands on her waist and said, "All right. I'll say one-two-three-go, then you sort of leap and I'll help you the rest of the way."

Sophie took a shuddering breath and nodded, unable to speak. How was she going to keep this trip innocent when his big hands made her waist seem tiny, and having his fingers curled around her middle so intimately also felt—right. Wonderful. Perfect.

"One-two-three-go!"

With one foot in the stirrup, she pushed off with the one still on the ground. When she got about halfway up, Jeb pressed his palms to her bottom to give her a boost and her mind went blank. She forgot the part about swinging her leg around and nearly went flying headfirst over the horse. She screamed, stopping her out-of-control forward momentum by slapping her palms on the saddle, which caused her to fall backward, almost on top of Jeb.

Knowing he was probably furious she quickly said, "I forgot the thing about swinging my leg around."

"Well, don't forget this time!"

His angry voice caused her to face him. "Hey! Don't yell! I'm new at this."

But when she caught his gaze, his eyes were bright and aware, taut with male need. Everything she felt from the touch of his hands on her was magnified a hundredfold in his eyes.

He very quietly said, "Let's try this again."

She almost told him to forget the ride. Not only was she still on the ground and still in need of his hands on her waist to hoist her up again, but she didn't think her plan to stay neutral, like a boss and his housekeeper, was going to work. Their attraction was too strong and they were about to take a ride, alone.

Thinking of the two of them all by themselves in the wide-open spaces brought a million possibilities to mind—including the fact that he could absolutely ignore her for hours. But she didn't think so. If just having his hands on her behind caused her to forget everything but her name, out there in the wilderness, with no one to see, and the real world so far behind them, it was more likely that their attraction would get the better of them and one of them would act on it.

Then what would she do? If he was the one to lose control would she resist? *Could* she resist? If he kissed her, would she let him touch her? And if he touched her, would she be able to stop them from making love? All this time she'd been so sure she could keep herself in line, but what if she only kept her wits because he kept his? And what if he only kept his because of prying eyes? What if, totally and completely alone, they couldn't resist the force that made her shiver with need?

He turned her around to face the horse again, grabbed her foot and tucked it in the stirrup. Before she could argue or even get her bearings, he said, "One, two, three go!"

Rather than give her time to launch her leg over the horse, he put one hand on her butt to boost her at the same time that he grabbed her leg and helped it over the saddle. In what seemed like three seconds, she was straddling the mare.

Excitement raced through her and she forgot everything she'd been worrying about. "I did it!"

He shook his head with a snort. "Yeah. It's more like *I* did it."

"What does it matter?" Atop the mare—who might look small next to Jeb's horse, but who made Sophie feel as if she were sitting on top of the world—Sophie experienced a wave of sheer power. *This*—this feeling of power and control—was probably part of the draw of working on a ranch, but it was probably also the reason Jeb didn't appear concerned about their alone time. With this high view of the world, she genuinely believed she was strong enough to do anything. Including resist her boss.

Jeb led the way, his horse walking at a leisurely pace. Not yet accustomed to straddling the huge beast, Sophie swayed from side to side, thanking God Jeb was in front and couldn't see her.

"You better find your center. Get yourself settled."

"Do you have a rearview mirror or something?"

"I just know how greenhorns sit."

Irritated that he'd called her a greenhorn, even though she was, Sophie fidgeted until she stabilized. The mare glanced back at her as if voicing her approval. Sophie totally relaxed.

In only a few minutes they left behind the ranch buildings, and were riding a dirt trail. Leaving the hustle and bustle of Jeb's business, they rode into silence. Sunshine reflected off green grass with a dark mountain backdrop.

After a while, Sophie could no longer stay silent. "This is spectacular."

He half turned. "The view?"

"The whole thing. The view. The peace and quiet. The privacy." She peeked over at him. "When you're guaranteed that your mother's students will fill up the downstairs of your house every day, privacy becomes very important."

"Nowhere to run?"

"No. I could always find a place to run and even more places to hide. That was the problem. I would have spent my teen years in a closet."

He laughed. "*Would* have?"

"Julianna, our housekeeper, typically found me and put me to work."

For that he turned. "Really?"

"I think she knew what my parents refused to see."

He slowed his horse, allowing her to catch up with him. "What's that?"

"That we weren't really rich. I don't think she was trying to teach me a skill for a job, but she recognized that I'd need to know how to scrub my own kitchen and dust a bedroom."

"And you turned those few lessons into a career."

"You scoff, but because this job had room and board, the money I made here would have paid off the hospital and doctor bills from Brady's birth in no time."

He looked away, obviously uncomfortable, but Sophie wouldn't take the comment back or even amend it. She wasn't sorry he now knew how much this job had meant to her, and even mentioning Brady might have been for the best. He didn't like kids and she had one. That had cooled his attraction every time.

They rode for another ten minutes in silence. She hadn't intended to insult him because the silence was strained, oppressive. Even meaningless small talk would be better than this.

She took a breath and casually said, "What brought *you* here?"

"What makes you think I'm not from here?"

"Slim and the other guys talk with a barely discernible twang, but still with a distinct way of speaking. You don't have one." She waited a beat then said, "So where are you from?"

"Nowhere."

She laughed. "Right. Everybody hates their roots, but a person can't claim not to have any."

"I can. My parents were everything your parents pretended to be. Rich. Sophisticated. Jet-setters."

Her eyes widened. "No kidding."

"They had so much money they didn't need to put on airs or even stay in one place. They lived where they wanted, did what they wanted when they wanted."

"And ignored you?" she asked, almost hoping he'd say yes because then they'd be kindred spirits.

He shook his head. "No such luck. I was on every fishing boat, at every party, on every yacht."

She gaped at him, angry that he didn't appreciate his good fortune. "Pardon me for not being sympathetic."

He laughed. "Right. It was a joy to be exposed to things a kid shouldn't see."

She'd never thought of that. Adults partying on a yacht probably forgot to be discreet. She pictured pitchers of margaritas, bikini clad women and men ogling, maybe getting a little free with their hands.

Jeb pulled on his horse's reins. "Let's stop for a minute, give the horses a chance to get a drink."

He'd brought them to a small stream that wound through a grove of trees. Sophie gazed around in awe. "Okay."

He easily dismounted. Sophie watched him then mimicked what he had done.

"Hey, look at that." She grinned. "I got myself down."

"The trick will be whether or not you can get yourself back up."

She laughed, but her laughter suddenly faded. He was nice, funny even. Fun to be with. It was hard to believe he didn't like kids. Especially since he supported an orphanage. Why would a man who didn't like kids support an orphanage?

In the ensuing silence, she glanced around, rummaging in her brain for something to say and remembering he'd never really finished the explanation about his childhood. "So, with such wacky parents, how'd you grow up to be so normal?"

He grabbed the reins of both horses and walked them to the stream. As they drank, he said, "I didn't. I was the most confused person on the planet until I went to university. I lived on campus for the first two years, but eventually I got an apartment next door to some really stable guys. People who were in school because they needed to learn accounting and business practices and even history."

"Let me guess…ranchers?"

"Yes." He glanced over. "As soon as the horses are done drinking, we'll turn back."

"But we hardly went anywhere!"

"We've gone far enough."

Yeah. They'd gone far enough in the conversation! He'd told her a bit of his past but this was as far as he intended to go. And the only reason she could think of why he'd refuse to tell her facts so far from the past that they shouldn't matter anymore was that they did matter. Which meant school or his friends somehow connected to one of their two taboo topics. Their attraction or her baby.

Curiosity tingled through her. How could friends cause a man to dislike kids? It didn't make any sense. And because his dislike of kids had cost her her job, she couldn't let it go.

She walked over to him. "You know what? I don't think so. Everybody else might have to scrape and bow when you talk, but I'm already fired. So I'm not taking no for an answer. I want to hear about the guys who impressed you enough that you copied them."

He sighed. "No."

She groaned. "Why not? What's the big deal in telling me?"

"It's none of your business."

"Really? I'm guessing the reason you don't like kids is all wrapped up in this story, and since I lost this job because you don't like kids, I think I have the right to know."

He turned away, but she caught his arm and spun him around again. "What are you so afraid of?"

His gaze latched onto hers, his stormy eyes revealing his anger. "Seriously, you don't want to mess with this right now."

"Yes, I do! And I'm not going to stop—"

As quickly as she'd spun him around, he grabbed her by the waist and hauled her against him, his lips falling to hers. He didn't kiss her gently like a man expressing an emotion. He kissed her roughly like a man in the grip of a need. He swallowed her gasp of surprise and took advantage of the slight parting of her lips to slide his tongue into her mouth. Her head spun and liquid warmth fell from her chest to her toes.

But she didn't stop him. The same thing that had its hooks in him took a hold of her. Her mind went blissfully black and she kissed him back, every bit as greedy as he was.

He abruptly pulled away, his breathing raspy, his voice equally so when he said, "Now, can we go back?"

She stared into his stormy-gray eyes. Saw the heat, but also the confusion. He hadn't kissed her to demonstrate their attraction. He was warning her. Their chemistry was a little too hot and a little too strong. At some point it would get the better of them. If they didn't stop talking, getting close, that "point" would be today.

"Yes. We can go back."

But could they?

CHAPTER SEVEN

A LITTLE after eight the next morning, the kitchen door swung open. Sophie peeked up from feeding Brady to see Jeb stopped in the doorway. Their gazes caught. The same syrupy warmth that had flooded her when he kissed her poured through her, but he hardly registered a reaction. If anything, he looked confused.

Quickly glancing down again, she saw the baby spoon in her hand, remembered Brady was right beside her in the chair and her heart stopped. Jeb liked her well enough—maybe too well—when they were alone. When it was just them. A man and a woman who were incredibly sexually attracted. But put Brady into the picture and he had absolutely no interest in her.

He walked directly to the coffeepot. "I got a call about three o'clock this morning.

Slim's mom had a heart attack. He's in Texas. He'll be out for a while."

Sophie's breath backed up in her lungs. Sympathy for Slim enveloped her, along with sudden understanding. Jeb's confusion had nothing to do with her or Brady. "Oh, my goodness, I'm so sorry."

"Yeah. He's a mess." Jeb filled his travel mug with coffee and faced her. "He called me as soon as he got off the phone with his sister, borrowed the plane and flew down." His gaze found Brady and his eyes narrowed. She expected him to chastise her, but he kept the conversation on Slim. "I imagine he's pacing a hospital corridor about now."

His eyes flicked back to Sophie, and she tried not to feel anything when their gazes met, but a wave of sensation rolled through her. She couldn't turn off or tone down her re-actions to him. She'd never felt any of the things with Mick that she'd experienced the day before when Jeb had kissed her. Her off-the-charts response to him was confusing, frustrating, seductive—and absolutely insane.

The man didn't even want to be in the same room with her son and she suspected he wasn't saying anything about Brady right now only because he had more pressing concerns. She couldn't possibly be attracted to someone who disliked her baby so much that he wouldn't keep her as his housekeeper. So why had her heart flip-flopped and her chest tightened, just because he looked at her? Hadn't she already made this mistake with Mick?

"Can you manage without him for a few days?"

She shook her head as if to clear a haze. "I'm sorry. I missed what you said."

"I asked if you could manage without Slim for a few days."

She hesitated. Furniture would begin arriving today. Slim had assigned two hands to help her, but she had no idea if two men would be enough. Still, Jeb's plate was full. She wouldn't add to his stress.

"Yes. I can manage."

Jeb shook his head. "That pause you took says you're not sure you can."

"I'm not. I don't know how much of the furniture will get here today. And we're also on a deadline. Every pair of hands helps."

"Okay, see how it goes and if you need more men, don't pussyfoot around, ask."

She nodded. He snapped the lid on his

travel mug and left the kitchen. Sophie let out her breath. She had to get a hold of herself. Not only was her attraction to Jeb so strong it was frightening, but she had to work here for another two weeks. If nothing else, she had to keep her reactions to herself. With Slim gone Jeb didn't need the added burden of having to tiptoe around her. If anything, she should find a way to pitch in and help.

It didn't take much thinking to figure out what she could do. Though Jeb had told her dinner was no longer her responsibility, with the change in his workload all bets were off. Nine chances out of ten he wouldn't have time to get his own supper and if she fixed him something, he'd appreciate it.

The question was could they handle being in the same room for twenty or so minutes while he ate?

Furniture began arriving at noon. The two men Slim had assigned to her, Bob and Monty, assisted the delivery men with unloading trucks and carted the sofas and chairs, boxes and crates to rooms Sophie designated. They didn't unpack anything, merely got everything to its proper place, knowing they'd have their work cut out for them the following day.

In between deliveries, Sophie put a pan of three-cheese ziti in the oven. She wouldn't beg Jeb to eat. If he refused dinner, she would simply smile and let him go his own way. But her conscience wouldn't let her shirk her responsibility in a time when everybody should be pitching in.

At dark, Jeb entered the kitchen, his face drawn and tired. The steps he took were slow. He even closed the door softly, as if he barely had any energy.

Sophie turned to the stove, making her appearance in the kitchen as casual, normal, as possible. They were supposed to be housekeeper and boss, not potential lovers. She'd already proven that when she behaved professionally, he did, too, so maybe if she stuck to that principle, he'd follow suit.

Her back to him as she stirred, she said, "Have you had supper?"

"No."

"Good. I made three-cheese ziti." She faced him again and smiled cautiously. "It's one of my specialties. I could have it on the table in ten minutes, if you're interested."

For a few seconds he didn't reply. Sophie held her breath. She knew he was thinking about that kiss, about their attraction, about whether or not spending this much time alone was a good idea. She couldn't believe he was so afraid of being alone with her that he'd go hungry rather than let her cook for him but she also didn't really know him. And that was another thing she had to remember when their attraction began to get the best of her.

Finally he said, "I don't have to eat in the dining room, do I?"

"It's easier for me if you eat in the kitchen."

"Can I clean up first?"

"Sure. That'll give me time to toss a salad."

He left the kitchen and Sophie sucked in a breath. Her preparing supper for him was the right thing to do. If they behaved like a normal boss and housekeeper, it might also be a way for them to get beyond the attraction neither one of them wanted.

But just as she grabbed the pot holders to pull the ziti from the oven, Brady's soft cries issued from the baby monitor and she froze.

Oh, no!

She raced to her crying baby, hoping she could coax him back to sleep before Jeb returned from cleaning up, but from the way he bounced and yelped when she entered the bedroom she knew he was too awake to drift back to sleep with a back rub. And she didn't have time to rock him.

She glanced from the door to the crib and back again. She had no choice. She had to take Brady to the high chair.

Jeb walked into the kitchen to find Sophie busy at the stove. He pulled a chair away from the table and immediately noticed the baby in the high chair beside it. The kid grinned up at him.

He pulled in a silent breath. This had to have been the worst day of his life. Not only was his foreman gone and his ranch in total confusion, but he'd spent the day thinking about a kiss that had been a whopper of a mistake. Now, he had a baby six inches away from him.

But just like everything else that had happened in the past fifteen hours, even this meal wasn't part of the agenda. Having the little boy at the table must have been unavoidable, or Sophie wouldn't have him here. The woman had done nothing but try to please him since she'd arrived at the Silver

Saddle. Tonight she'd been ready with supper—even though he hadn't asked. Surely, he could muster twenty minutes of civility for her baby?

He glanced over.

The kid grinned again.

His lungs felt as if they had filled with cement, but he refused to give into the sorrow, the loss, the self-pity. None of his troubles were this baby's fault.

"Hey…" He paused. What had Slim called him? Brody? Bradley? *Brady*. "Hey, Brady."

The little boy pounded his rattle on the high chair tray.

Sophie brought a salad to the table and this time when Jeb's heart turned over in his chest it was for an entirely different reason. His blood hadn't ever boiled in his veins the way it had from a thirty-second kiss meant to dissuade himself and the woman setting a salad in front of him. He'd wanted to show her they shouldn't play with fire, and all he'd accomplished was to throw gas on the flames.

With the salad in front of him, Sophie headed back to the stove. He squeezed his eyes shut, told himself he was thirty-five years old, owner of a thriving business, too smart to let a little thing like emotion ruin his plans.

"I'm sorry that I had to bring Brady to the kitchen. He was sleeping and I thought he was down for the night, but—"

Jeb stopped her with a wave of his hand. "It's fine."

She sucked in a relieved breath. "Thanks. I'm sorry—"

Yet another apology from a woman who really hadn't done anything wrong. Her fear of him shamed him. Life had treated this woman abysmally. He knew it. Now he was adding to her misery. "Don't say you're sorry. This is fine. I'm fine. We're all fine."

"Okay."

A few seconds passed in silence as he grabbed a dinner roll and buttered it. The baby pounded his rattle on the tray. Made soft cooing noises. Laughed at nothing.

From the stove, Sophie called, "Are you having fun back there?"

He giggled.

Jeb put another pat of butter on his roll, desperately trying to ignore them.

But when she came to the table with a bowl of green beans, she looked at Jeb, not the baby.

"Can I ask you a question?"

The loner in him, the man who'd realized five years ago when Laine had left him that he'd always be alone, wanted to say no. But his fair side, the part of him that knew just how wrong it was to make a woman feel embarrassed for her child, wouldn't let him. He focused on his roll. "Sure. You can ask a question."

"What is it about babies that you don't like?"

His knife stopped. She'd gone straight for the jugular. The moment of truth. The point where he either spilled his guts or gave her just enough of an answer to satisfy her curiosity.

He cleared his throat. No matter how much he wanted to be fair, the bottom line truth she was digging for wasn't any of her business. So, he simply said, "I don't dislike babies. I just haven't been around them much."

"Oh."

He dug into his salad.

"Because of your parents' lifestyle?"

He nodded.

"Not a lot of people with kids on yachts?"

"Not a lot of people who live to party actually have kids. And if they do, they're typically hidden away with a nanny."

"Do you ever wish you'd been left with a nanny?"

He had. A million times over he'd wished his parents had purchased a home. *Anywhere.* In the country. In the city. Anywhere. They could have even left him with a nanny. They could have left him with an army of nannies and he wouldn't have cared because he could have consistently attended school, made friends, known stability. Then he wouldn't have made his mistake with Laine. He wouldn't have hurt her or himself. He wouldn't have the feeling he was tumbling over a waterfall every time he looked at the woman serving him dinner.

But, again, that was his private misery. Not something he'd share with a woman he'd known about a week, a woman who'd be leaving his ranch in another two.

"My parents did what they did. I learned long ago not to wish for things that didn't or can't happen." Before she could ask another question, he quickly said, "What about you? Have you ever wished you'd married Brady's dad?"

It was a low blow to turn the tables so harshly, but when she paused and licked her lips, Jeb forgot all about Brady's dad and her possible reply. His gaze fell to her mouth and he remembered every second of kissing her. The fire in his blood. The silkiness of her lips. The way they seemed to fit together so perfectly.

"Like every unmarried pregnant woman, I thought getting married would solve all our problems. So, yeah, at first I did wish I could have married Brady's dad." She rolled her eyes. "Boy, would *that* have been a mistake!"

"What was he like?" Jeb asked, hoping against hope she'd tell him that her ex was just like him so he could easily talk himself out of liking her, wanting her.

"He was very focused."

"Really?" Apparently he and her ex *were* alike. "Was he building a business or something?"

"He was building a life. He had a great job, made lots of money and could afford to have absolutely anything he wanted. So what he was doing was creating a lifestyle, a home."

Jeb frowned. From everything he'd seen, Sophie was exactly the kind of woman a man would want to create a home with. What she planned to do with his house was magazine worthy. So her boyfriend dumping her didn't make any sense.

"If he was building a life I'm not sure I understand how you didn't fit."

"Oh, I fit," she readily replied. "It was Brady who didn't."

Jeb's heart flopped over in his chest and he glanced at the perfect, happy boy in the high chair. Righteous indignation exploded in him for the child unwanted by his dad and he could have happily found the man and beat him to a pulp. But even as part of him condemned Brady's dad, the other part reminded him that he wasn't any better. And *that,* the truth he avoided more than confronted, was his real avenue to obliterate his longing for a relationship between him and his housekeeper. And maybe it was time he not only faced it, but also he gave her enough of a hint that she'd get the stars out of her eyes, too.

He cleared his throat. "The truth is, Sophie, some people aren't cut out to be fathers."

"That's what Mick said."

Jeb waited a beat, then another, until she returned to the table with a glass of iced tea. When her gaze found his, he quietly said, "I'm not, either."

He saw from the way her eyes sharpened, then darkened, that she got his message. Women with babies shouldn't get too attached to men who weren't cut out to be fathers. Though he'd been subtly telling her that by his behavior since the moment she pulled Brady from her car, saying the words aloud pounded home the point.

She stiffened and shifted ever so slightly, putting herself between him and her son, as if protecting him, and he got *her* message. Her baby would always take precedence. Especially over something as fleeting as a potential romance.

Good for her.

He ate the rest of his dinner in near silence, while Sophie puttered behind him, storing leftovers, stacking dishes in the dishwasher. When they did talk it was about Slim's mother's upcoming surgery. Sophie volunteered to call her father and get background information about the procedure, but Jeb reminded her that he could look it up on the Internet, closing the door because he didn't want to get cozy with her. He didn't want to depend on her for personal things. Hell, he didn't even want to have personal discussions with her. He just wanted to be left alone.

After the main course, he refused cobbler and walked out of the kitchen as if nothing major had happened between them. But as he strode through the downstairs corridor to the stairway that led to the family room and ultimately the weight room, he knew that was a lie. Something major had happened. She hadn't merely cooked for him. They'd talked and he'd told her something he hadn't ever told anyone else.

But it had been unavoidable. They had to deal with their attraction once and for all. They'd hit the point where he had to come right out and say he wasn't cut out to be a dad, so there'd be no more guessing. No more confusion. No more wondering. She'd simply stay away.

It was exactly what he wanted.

So, why did he feel so awful?

As he passed the hall closet on his way to change into sweats to exercise, he noticed the door was ajar. With an absent movement, he raised his arm to close it, but as he did he saw a swatch of pink and he stopped.

Seeing the box of things Laine had left

behind, his entire body hummed with emotion. Anger. Sadness. Anticipation. Wishing. Hoping.

Not wanting to go down that road again, he tried to close the door, but the corner of the box hung out, over the thin metal runner for the sliding panel. That's why the door wouldn't close. Somebody had been in here.

Sophie.

She knew there had been a woman in his life. One of the men might even have mentioned that Jeb had been married before.

He stifled a groan. No wonder she'd been so quiet when he'd told her he wasn't cut out to be a dad. She'd probably been jumping to all kinds of conclusions. She might have even envisioned a sad wife, longing for children, leaving because Jeb refused to have any.

Damn Laine for leaving these things.

Steeled for a rush of pain, Jeb stooped beside the box. He looked down at the pink weights, pink towels, pink everything. He pictured Laine working out, using the weights, laughing as they ran side by side on the treadmills, drying off with one of the hideous pink towels.

He picked up the weight, forced himself to

feel it, to remember the sound of it crashing through the mirrored wall across from the weight bench.

Pain strong enough that she'd lost her temper, lost control and done something she never would have done in a million years. Just as she'd said things that she never would have even contemplated had their situation not been so heartrending.

That's why he wouldn't even consider exploring his feelings for Sophie. He wouldn't put Sophie through the kind of emotional pain that arose when a woman got involved with him.

After dressing herself and Brady the next morning, Sophie made her way to the kitchen, where she found Jeb leaning against the counter, waiting for the coffee to brew.

She paused in the doorway, not sure if she should pretend she forgot something and leave before he made an issue of Brady being in the same room, or push the envelope. The night before he hadn't minded Brady being at the table. After a bit of hemming and hawing around, he had admitted he wasn't cut out to be a father, but, oddly, that had actually made sense of many things. A man who supported an orphanage couldn't possibly be opposed to a baby, but he might worry that with a fatherless kid underfoot he'd be forced into the role of surrogate dad. A role he didn't want.

"I started the coffee."

She took a cautious step into the room. "So I see."

He turned to the counter, reached for something on the other side of the coffeepot and faced her again, displaying the pink weight she'd found in the box of junk in the gym.

"There's a box of this stuff in the closet in front of the weight room shower. It belonged to my ex-wife. Have one of the boys put it out in the trash barrel."

She said, "Okay," but her mind was going a million miles a second. Not because he'd admitted he'd been married before, but because he still wasn't reacting to Brady. Did this mean that with his objection to being cast in the role of father out in the open, he now didn't mind being around Brady—as long as she didn't try to get him to play daddy?

She took a few careful steps into the

kitchen, walking to the cabinet where she stored Brady's cereal. Unfazed, Jeb turned to open the cupboard door above the coffee-maker. He pulled down his travel mug and poured in cream, as if it were any other morning. Nothing wrong. Nothing amiss.

He *didn't* mind having her baby in the room!

The coffeemaker groaned and he picked up the coffeepot to fill his travel mug.

With her baby on her hip, she walked to the refrigerator to grab the milk to make Brady's cereal, still watching Jeb out of her peripheral vision, checking for any sign that he wanted her baby gone. But as she opened the refrigerator door, she caught him staring at Brady with a look of longing so intense it nearly stole her breath.

She ducked into the refrigerator before he realized she'd seen it, but that expression totally confused her. That was the look of a man who loved kids. Yearned for kids. Not a guy who didn't want to be a dad. How could he believe he wasn't cut out to be a father?

Pulling out of the refrigerator, she glanced at the pink weight. Maybe it wasn't a coinci-dence that after spending time with Brady the night before Jeb had been thinking of his ex-wife, maybe even deliberately going through her old workout gear? Thanks to Mick, she knew that people sometimes said terrible things to each other when a relationship was breaking down. Maybe, disillusioned over their failed marriage, Jeb's wife had told him he wouldn't make a good dad?

Telling herself that was none of her business, Sophie set the milk on the counter and reached into the cupboard for a bowl. After placing it on the countertop, she shifted to the drawer to retrieve a spoon, and again caught Jeb gazing at her son.

That absolutely was *not* the look of a guy who wasn't daddy material. If the expression on his face was anything to go by, he longed to hold her son.

Taking the cereal ingredients to the table, she told herself to let it go, but it was no use. The man was curious about her baby. Wanted to hold him. Maybe even get to know him. But he wouldn't ask, and after his declaration that he wasn't cut out to be a dad, she couldn't make the offer.

She frowned. Maybe offering to let him hold her son wasn't the way to go about this.

If she made it seem as if he was doing her a favor by holding Brady, he probably wouldn't think twice about it.

Before she lost her courage, she turned to Jeb and asked, "Would you hold him while I mix his cereal?"

Without giving him a chance to question if he could handle it, she shoved Brady at him. He grasped the baby around his tummy. "Wait. Stop. I can't—"

Sophie turned away, busying herself with the cereal and jar of strained fruit. "Sure you can. Just put his butt on your forearm and he'll settle in himself. Remember what you told me about finding my center on the horse. It's sort of the same principle."

She glanced over out of the corner of her eye, ready to spring into action if Jeb bobbled her baby. Looking simultaneously horrified and terrified, Jeb quickly did as she instructed. Within seconds Brady was comfortably nestled on his arm and against his chest. Jeb put his big hand across the baby's back, securing him.

Sophie relaxed, but she prepared Brady's cereal quickly, not wanting to test Jeb's abilities or his patience. When everything was ready, she pulled the baby from Jeb's arms and carried him to the high chair.

Jeb picked up his coffee. Several seconds ticked off the clock in total silence. But he didn't leave the kitchen. He wasn't scowling. If he was really angry, he would have stormed out of the room. Wouldn't he?

"So he likes that mush?"

Sophie smiled. He wasn't angry. And he was curious. "Yes. He loves this mush."

"What is it?"

"Rice cereal and strained fruit." She lifted the jar and examined it. "Bananas today."

"I'm guessing it tastes better than it looks."

She laughed. "It does."

"I hope so." He turned to the counter again, found the lid for his travel mug and snapped it on before heading for the door, where he paused. "You wouldn't mind making supper again?"

"No. I love to cook."

"Okay, then I'll see you later."

When he was gone, Sophie let out the breath she had been holding. They might not ever get together romantically. Her leaving precluded that, but she had the sudden, intense feeling that that didn't matter. Jeb

Worthington was a nice guy, who supported an orphanage, who believed, for some reason, that he'd make a lousy father. She understood accusations being hurled by an angry lover. She understood believing them, if only because of being vulnerable in the moment. But Jeb had been divorced a while. It was time for him to get beyond the accusations. And happy Brady was maybe just the baby to help him along.

After breakfast, Sophie found Monty and Bob waiting in the downstairs family room for her. Mug of coffee in one hand, Brady on her arm, she greeted them. "Good morning."

Monty took off his hat. Bob blushed endearingly. "Morning."

Maneuvering through stacks of boxes, she said, "Okay, nearly everything has arrived for this room and today we're going to pull it together."

Monty's eyes widened. "Please tell me we don't have to get that sofa up that thin stairwell."

Sophie glanced at the "S" shaped monstrosity that had been in the room when she arrived. "Nope, I decided to keep it." She walked to the play yard, which she'd taken from the office and set up in the corner of the big room the day before. Sliding Brady inside, she said, "But we do have to move it to the middle of the room."

Monty frowned. "The middle of the room?"

"We have to surround it with color. Otherwise, no matter where we try to hide it, it will stick out like a sore thumb."

She pointed across the room. "See that big long tube over there?"

Bob nodded.

"That's the rug that goes under it."

"Under it?" Bob and Monty said in unison. But Bob added, "We're going to need another pair of hands."

Sophie looked around. "Actually another pair of hands isn't a bad idea." Jeb had told her that if she needed help, she shouldn't pussyfoot around. So, she wouldn't. "Bob, why don't you go ask Mr. Worthington to join us?"

His eyes grew large and his mouth fell open. "Jeb?"

"Yes."

He pulled in a breath. "Okay, but he isn't going to like this."

"What he'll like is the beautiful home he'll

have to show his potential clients," she reminded Bob with another smile. "Seriously. This is important."

"Okay."

Bob left and Sophie and Monty worked at unpacking lamps, artwork and other accessories for the room. Within ten minutes, Jeb was clomping down the stairway with Bob.

Before he could say anything, Sophie said, "Thank goodness you could help us. This room is huge, but the couch is a dinosaur. We definitely need you if we're going to have this space ready for your clients."

Knowing he wouldn't argue that, Sophie smiled. Jeb scowled. "With Slim out of town, I'm swamped."

She knew that but she also knew that the only private time she'd have to show Jeb he could be okay with kids would be when Slim was gone.

"Well, we could spend the next ten minutes arguing over why you should help us. Or we could just get everything moved so you can leave."

"Fine. Whatever. Let's get started already."

She directed Bob and Monty to the left side of the sectional sofa. "You guys move that over there," she said, pointing to the far corner. "Jeb and I will position this section in the center of the room."

Bob and Monty nodded. As she and Jeb shifted the center curve of the sofa to the right, the two cowboys walked the bottom of the "S" shape out of the way.

She brushed off her hands and stood back to examine the center placement. "That's it. That's exactly where the sofa belongs."

"Great," Jeb said, heading for the stairway.

"Oh, no," Sophie scolded. "Not yet! We have to get the rug in place, and then put the sofa on top of it, then you can go."

Jeb sighed.

Sophie assigned him to help Bob remove the bold print rug from its shipping container. Blocks of burgundy, brown, beige and gold brightened the hardwood floor when they rolled it out. Sophie and Monty placed the center curve of the white "S" on the left end of the rug. Then Jeb and Monty returned the bottom of the "S" to its place beside the center of the sectional sofa.

With the big "S" in place, Sophie instructed Jeb and Bob to maneuver other furniture around it but suddenly Brady began to fuss.

Sophie turned to Monty. "See if he'll take a rattle."

Monty scurried to the play yard. He picked up a rattle and shoved it at Brady who only fussed all the more.

Jeb sighed again. "Let me." He grabbed the rattle from Monty's hands, shook it to make the pleasant sound and smiled down at Brady. "Here, little guy."

Sophie held back a smile. He was a natural with kids! She couldn't believe his ex-wife had somehow convinced him he wasn't cut out to be a father. From here on out, she would expose him to Brady every chance she got, until he realized how wrong he was to believe that.

Brady sniffed and stopped crying, but he didn't take the rattle from Jeb. Seeing another opportunity, Sophie called, "Can you pick him up?" from the other side of the room, where she was holding a picture for Monty to hang. "As soon as I'm done here, I'll take him upstairs."

Jeb reached down and lifted Sophie's son. As inconspicuously as possible, she watched him settle Brady on his arm just as she'd shown him only a few hours before in the kitchen.

It was everything Sophie could do not to laugh out loud. Getting Jeb accustomed to her baby, and beyond the belief that he wasn't cut out to be a dad, would be a piece of cake.

When Jeb arrived in the kitchen for supper, Sophie and Brady were already there. That didn't surprise him. Neither did her request that he hold Brady while she tossed a salad. He glanced over at the empty high chair, knowing that's where Brady should have been and pulled in a resigned breath.

He could come right out and confront her about challenging his statement, except he didn't think she was forcing him to interact with Brady out of a challenge. At least not a romantic one. He didn't have the sense that she was trying to prove to him that he could get along with Brady to obliterate his excuse for not wanting to get involved with her. She'd hardly looked at him all day—except to boss him around. Now that he was okay with her baby, it almost seemed she wasn't interested.

Realizing just how "okay" he was with the little boy, Jeb felt a rush of happiness. He had to admit that now that he'd held the little guy without disastrous consequences, he didn't have to run anymore if the baby was around. Actually he could probably enjoy this baby.

The idea brought him up short. He'd never even considered "enjoying" Brady. But he knew he would. And when he recognized that, he realized something that stunned him.

Technically he no longer had an excuse for wanting Sophie off his ranch.

He frowned, wondering if she'd gotten him accustomed to her baby just to keep her job. But curiosity about her motives took a back seat to the sudden vision he had of what life would be like if Sophie stayed on with her little boy. Jeb would probably be the one to take the kid out to see the ranch. He'd be the one to teach Brady to ride. Actually, if Sophie stayed long enough he could take this little boy under his wing. Teach him the ropes of being a man.

The joy that rose in him at just the thought of "playing" dad caused him to swallow hard and squeeze his eyes shut with pain. How foolish, how needy, to so desperately long to use someone else's child as if he were his own.

He set Brady in his high chair. "I need to wash up."

He refused to be so pathetic that he'd settle for a few months or a few years being the pretend dad to his housekeeper's son.

At this point in his life he had little more than his pride. He wasn't giving up that, too.

CHAPTER EIGHT

AFTER dinner, Sophie cleaned the kitchen then returned to the basement room, Brady on her arm.

Lowering him into the play yard, she said, "I know you're getting tired, but you need to stay up another hour in order to sleep through the night. So I might as well try to get a little more work done."

He gooed up at her. She smiled. "You are adorable."

He giggled.

She ran her fingers through the downy hair on his head, ruffling it even more. "You better hope that mane of yours tames before you're a teenager."

He giggled again.

"I'm serious. That could be a definite handicap with the girls."

"What could be a handicap with the girls?"

Hearing Jeb's comment, she glanced up and saw him coming down the stairs. She straightened away from the play yard and their eyes met across the huge room.

Subdued yellow linen curtains now matched the yellow in the multicolored throw pillows piled on the sofa and chairs. A sun-shaped clock smiled from above the fireplace mantel. Books and wood sculptures filled the wall unit.

Fearing his reaction to the nearly finished room, Sophie swallowed before answering his question. "His hair. If it doesn't settle down a bit before he hits his teen years he could be in real trouble."

Jeb laughed and said, "No doubt about it." Then he glanced around.

Sophie didn't know if he'd come down to inspect the job she was doing or if he was on his way to his workout room, but whatever his reason, he was here. Seeing a nearly finished room. About to pronounce judgment.

"I like it."

"Really?" Her heart began beating again. "The yellow doesn't put you off?"

"It's not my favorite color, but I'm guessing the other colors—" He pointed to the bur-gundy, brown, yellow and burnt orange throw pillows "—like the ones in those pillows are so dark you felt you needed something to offset them."

She sagged with relief. "Exactly."

Silence descended on the room. Jeb didn't rush off as she expected him to. Instead he stood in the center of the room, looking uncharacteristically nervous.

He rubbed his hand along the back of his neck. "There's something else we need to discuss."

His ominous tone caused her to step back. "Okay."

"All along I've been saying you couldn't stay because of your baby, but with Slim gone and everything confused, I sort of got over that."

Her heart tripped over itself in her chest. That was not at all what she'd been expecting. "You did?"

"Yes. The kid's not really as much of a problem as I thought he was going to be."

"Are you saying I can stay?"

He met her gaze. "You've proven yourself. You fit here. And now I'm okay with the kid. So, yeah. I'd like you to stay. But there is a condition."

Stunned, Sophie could only nod.

"This is a business and I am your boss. And we've got to start acting more like that."

Though he didn't come right out and say it, she got his point. No more kisses on horse rides. Just the reminder of being in his arms that afternoon sent sensation careening through her, but she ignored it. The man did not want to be attracted to her and she needed this job. Agreeing to that was a no brainer.

"Okay."

"Another thing. Just because I'm in my house it doesn't mean my work is done for the day. I'm on the clock 24/7. Even when I'm not working, I'm thinking about work. That's how I get so much done in a day. You can't be handing your son to me. It's a distraction. He can be in the kitchen. When he gets older, he can roam around the house. But I don't want him underfoot. Understood?"

"Yes." For a home, a decent salary and benefits she'd be a fool to argue. "Understood."

"Good." He looked around. "Now, could you use some help?"

The change in his tone confused her as much as his question. "You just reminded me of how busy you are. Now, you're volunteering to help me?"

He laughed and Sophie gaped at him. But it suddenly sunk in that she was staying. *Staying.* She and this man would live together until she left his employ. It could be years. Hell, it could be *decades.* Now that the ground rules for her permanent employment had been laid. He was setting the tone.

"I might be busy, but this is my company. I have the most to gain from everything being done right. With you staying, I'll be around a little more often, checking into things."

Okay. She got it. And she could handle it. She could behave like an employee. No problem. "You're welcome to watch, but I'm only going to be putting on some finishing touches."

His gaze circled the room. "I'm not sure what kinds of touches you think the place still needs. It looks finished to me."

"Well, technically it is, but a few magazines on the table will help a woman to see herself relaxing down here." She pointed at the bar. "Cocktail glasses and some open liquor bottles will help a man to see himself standing behind the bar, mixing drinks.

Unless you have a few half-empty liquor bottles upstairs somewhere, I'm going to have to open those new bottles and toss a shot or two."

The look he gave her was half mortified, half shocked. "You're going to have a drink?"

She laughed. "No! I'm going to drain a bit off each bottle to make the liquor appear more inviting. Nobody wants to open the bottle, but if the bottle's already open, people will help themselves." She gazed around proudly. "I want this to be a help-yourself room. I want it to be ultracomfortable."

He looked around with her. "Okay. I buy it."

Brady began to fuss and Sophie sighed and walked over to him. She might be an employee, but she was also a mom. And it appeared this was the first test of that part of their arrangement.

"Well, that settles that. He's too tired to finish." She clapped her hands as a signal to Brady she would pick him up. "He has to go to bed."

She said the words casually, but out of the corner of her eye she watched Jeb to see how he would react to her leaving a project because of her baby.

His expression never changed. He didn't flinch. He didn't react at all. "Okay. See you in the morning."

Happiness exploded inside her. It was going to work! She could stop sassing. He could handle her baby. They could work together!

She lifted Brady out of the playpen, but as she turned toward the stairs, he dropped the little blue teddy bear he'd been chewing on.

Jeb was beside them in seconds, scooping it up. "Don't forget this."

Smiling, he handed the soft bear to her, but their fingers brushed and electricity danced up her arm. Their gazes caught and her heart skipped a beat.

But Jeb quickly turned away, adhering to their new condition that they behave more like a boss and housekeeper. And she agreed. She didn't know why he didn't want to be attracted to her, but she needed this job. She couldn't afford to be attracted to him any more than he wanted to be attracted to her.

She walked to the stairway. "I'll see you in the morning."

In her suite, she bathed Brady, slid him into pajamas and fed him a bottle while telling him a story. When he was done eating, he went out like a light.

Grabbing the baby monitor, she headed back to the basement. Though she'd given Jeb the impression that she was done for the day, that had only been a test. She needed to put the finishing touches on that room or she'd never get everything done before his clients arrived. It was only a little past eight. She had at least two hours she could work.

At the bottom of the stairs, she was surprised to see Jeb sitting at the bar.

He lifted his glass in salute then displayed a whiskey bottle that had been opened. "I found a way to help you."

She laughed. He was a funny guy. But she didn't think that's why he'd made the joke or stayed at the bar. They could make all the agreements they wanted about behaving like a boss and employee, but their electric moment earlier proved that their attraction wasn't going away just because they wanted it to. The only way to get over it or to learn to ignore it would be through practice.

And that, she guessed, was why he'd waited to see if she'd return.

"Very funny." She puffed a pillow. "Shouldn't you be on the treadmill by now?"

He swiveled on the bar stool. "I thought about it, but I also had a sneaking suspicion that after you put Brady to bed you'd come back down here." He nodded at the stepladder in the corner. "It's not good to be using one of those when you're alone. The shot of whiskey was just a perk."

She laughed again. "Seriously, I'm only going to be fluffing pillows and dusting."

He shrugged. "All right. I'll finish my drink and get out of your hair."

He took a small sip from the crystal glass and Sophie turned away, not surprised he intended to nurse his drink. He knew as well as she did that they had to get accustomed to each other.

Still, understanding what he was doing was one thing. Being successful at it was another. It wasn't exactly good practice to sit in the same room without talking. If they really wanted to get accustomed to each other, they had to talk. She just had to think of something normal to talk about. Brady was off-limits. They'd talked about him enough for now. Their attraction was taboo. She couldn't talk about the hands. Jeb wouldn't participate. She knew about his parents and childhood. He knew about hers.

She pulled in a breath. The topic range had slimmed to one not-exactly-spectacular subject. "My parents once had a male housekeeper."

He swiveled on his chair to face her, clearly glad she'd picked up the conversational ball. "Oh, yeah?"

"He taught me everything I know about decorating." Maintaining a casual tone, she stood in front of the sofa, studying the placement of a painting on the wall across from it. "He had a past a lot like mine. He learned to keep house and cook because both of his parents worked."

"Makes sense."

"The decorating thing just came naturally to him. He knew how to put furniture and accompanying pieces together in a room in such a way that they'd be stylish and still homey."

She turned just in time to see Jeb looking around again, obviously analyzing her placement of furniture and choice of accents. "If he taught you this," he said, motioning around the room, "he didn't need to go to school. He might have been just a guy who wanted to be comfortable."

She gazed around, too, trying to see the area from Jeb's perspective and realized that what he said was true. What she'd learned from Paul was how to make a space comfortable. Homey. Paul had wanted a stay-at-home mom and a dad who could have gone to his baseball games. Instead he had to cook, clean and do his own laundry *and* be his own cheerleader at Little League games. In a way, Paul had been as displaced as Jeb. And maybe that was why Jeb appreciated his style. They both wanted a home. And here she was creating one for Jeb.

Telling herself that turning Jeb's house into a home was her job and nothing else, she turned away and her eye caught the picture across from the sofa at another angle. Deciding she didn't like it, she grabbed the stepladder from the corner of the room where it had been stashed.

Settling it under the picture, she said, "It looks like you were right about the ladder."

"I knew the temptation to use it would be too strong."

She chuckled. "Right. I'm changing one little thing, not painting the entire room."

She climbed the two steps and lifted the picture from the wall, but it was heavier than she'd imagined. When she fully took its weight, she swayed and so did the ladder.

Jeb was beside her in seconds. He grabbed the picture, leaned it against the wall then caught her as she fell backward.

Sliding his one arm around her shoulders and the other beneath her knees, he swung her off her feet and away from the teetering ladder.

For several stunned seconds, she simply stared at him wide-eyed, her heart pounding from the near fall. Then she realized she was in his arms, cradled against his chest, and the pounding of her heart changed meaning. She'd never felt smaller or more feminine than she did right then. She was the woman making his home and he was her hero, her rescuer.

She stifled a groan. Why did she always think of him like this? Why couldn't he touch her without her brain hopping right over common sense and landing smack dab on a fantasy?

He set her on her feet, but they were standing face-to-face, so close their bodies almost touched.

This was not the way to get over an attraction.

Yet, she couldn't pull her eyes away from his. She couldn't take the step back that would have separated them.

And he couldn't, either. Several seconds passed in stunned silence then, as if in a trance, he began lowering his head to kiss her. Their gazes remained locked. They both knew what was happening. They both had several seconds to change their minds.

Neither did.

Their lips met softly. Warmly. Wetly. She closed her eyes, realizing how well they fit. How perfectly. Then all thought vanished in the wake of the landslide of feeling that tumbled through her. His kiss didn't merely convey the depth of his desire. A thread of genuine emotion wove through it. Where his physical needs had caused him to take in their first kiss, this time he gave. He pulled responses from her she didn't even know she was capable of giving, and once led down that path, her appetite was suddenly as strong as his.

Placing her hands on the sides of his face she brought him closer, her breasts crushed against his chest, and she deepened the kiss.

Intense emotion vibrated through her blood. Her pulse pounded. She pressed herself against him, wanting to be closer, feel more, take more, but he abruptly pulled away.

The breath heaved in both of their chests. Their gazes caught and clung. The silence in the room was thick, filled with unspoken questions.

He was the first to find his voice. "This isn't right."

Sophie touched her tingling lips. That kiss hadn't simply been a pulse-pounding exchange between two sexually attracted people. It had been an insight into how much he wanted her. He couldn't resist her any more than she could resist him. This attraction wasn't going away. In spite of their good intentions, it was somehow growing stronger.

Because she was getting to know him. His personality was now as much a part of the attraction as his sexuality. He was a nice guy. A smart man. A generous man who helped an orphanage. A logical man who had accepted her baby. How could she not want as much of him as he was willing to give her?

She cleared her throat. "It felt pretty right to me."

"No. It isn't. Not even a little bit."

She'd never been a bold person, but his kiss had filled her with courage. He more than wanted her. He *liked* her. And the only reason he'd given her that even hinted to why he didn't want to get involved was his fear that he wouldn't make a good dad. But in only two days she'd taken him from shying away from Brady to holding him while she finished dinner. Just as his reason for firing her was no longer valid, his reason for not wanting a relationship didn't wash, either.

She pulled in another breath, stilling her heart, calming her own hormones and spoke quietly, in truth. "Okay. I get that you don't want Brady underfoot. But you saw yourself with him today. He likes you and you're a natural."

He stepped away then turned away. "This isn't about Brady."

"I say it is."

"It isn't." He faced her again. "I don't want to hurt you."

She smiled. She'd never met a man so considerate of her feelings that he'd hurt her to prevent hurting her.

"How do you know you would?"

"I hurt my wife."

"From what you told me this morning, it sounded more like she hurt you."

"No. I hurt her." He pulled in a breath. "That's how I know I'll hurt you."

She honestly thought about that for a second, wondering if the angry statements of a wife losing her marriage could convince a good man he was bad. She couldn't see Jeb deliberately hurting anyone. Unless he had been preoccupied with the ranch? Slim had said ranch life was hard on marriages. So if Jeb had hurt his first wife it could have been through neglect.

"You didn't spend enough time with her?"

He laughed. "We were practically joined at the hip."

Which explained the side-by-side workout equipment, but also totally confused her. How could he hurt someone he had been so close to?

"Then I don't get it."

"Maybe you just need to believe me when I say I'm not cut out to be a husband?"

"Okay, that's enough. You can't be not cut out for everything. In fact, I don't believe you're not cut out to be a husband any more than I believe you're not cut out to be a father.

This very day you proved you could be a good dad. You were great with Brady."

"I never said I wasn't good with kids. I said I wasn't made to be a father."

Angry now because he seemed to be talking in circles, she gaped at him. "There's a difference?"

"Sophie, my wife left me because I couldn't give her the one thing she wanted more than her next breath. A child. It isn't that I simply decided one day that I wasn't the kind of guy to be a dad. Mother Nature told me I'd never be a dad. I can't have children."

CHAPTER NINE

SOPHIE froze, stunned into silence, and realized he'd been telling her this in one way, shape or form all along.

He stayed rooted to his spot, quietly waiting for her reaction, but words simply failed her. Of all things, she was sympathetic with his ex-wife. Now that she'd had a child, she knew she had been created just for that task. She *needed* children. She loved being a mom. As much as housekeeping gave her an income, being a mom gave her a reason to get up in the mornings.

Jeb took a step back, smiled ruefully. "Look, you're a wonderful mom. Brady's an adorable child. You should have more kids. Brady should have brothers and sisters. If you get involved with me those dreams end."

He caught her gaze, held it, the intensity in his eyes searing her with truth. "So let's not talk this to death. When I tell you getting involved with me would be the worst mistake of your life, just believe me."

The next morning, Jeb didn't immediately head for the kitchen and the coffeepot. Instead he slipped down a few hidden corridors finding the stairway to the basement. Though the family room Sophie had created was silent, he could still hear the echo of their voices as they talked the night before. Still feel the heat of his body's reactions as his mouth had mated with hers. Still feel the disappointment in her silence to his admission that he couldn't have kids.

That spoke louder than if she'd said a thousand words. A woman who had no real connection to her parents would want a family. Hell, he understood her need because *he'd* wanted a family. And Sophie was a wonderful mother. A good person. A generous, genuine woman. She deserved a family.

He should be glad she'd been stunned speechless. Every morning for the past five years he'd awakened wishing Laine had had the knowledge before she'd tumbled in love with him, created a life with him, and then had a doctor tell her he wasn't the man she'd assumed. At least Sophie had options. She might have come to the precipice with him, but there was no way he'd let her tumble over.

Unwittingly remembering the kiss again, he closed his eyes. He could feel her eager mouth beneath his, feel the impatient way she pressed herself against him.

He shook his head. He had to stop reliving that kiss. What he felt for her was wrong. And as soon as he punished his body with a good hour or two of exercise to get rid of the sexual tingle that still heated his blood, he would go into his kitchen, grab a mug of coffee and pretend he had absolutely no feelings for her.

He made it to the exercise room and performed a regimen of stretches to prepare for the real workout to come. After awakening his muscles, he sat on the weight bench. Every lift and movement required his full focus and attention, so he didn't have time to think about Sophie, about being attracted to her, about wanting more than what he knew he could legitimately have with her.

Yet, when he was done, when he'd punished himself for two grueling hours, she was the first thought to pop into his mind.

The tingle of need returned, along with it the usual arguments. He told himself that maybe he was jumping to conclusions. That maybe if he gave her a day to think about what he told her, she'd come around. Maybe her silence was actually a statement that she wanted time before she commented. Maybe after she thought things through, she'd decide having one child was enough.

And while she was malleable he could seduce her, bathe her with so much affection and attention that she wouldn't have time to get tangled up in the reality that she'd only be a mom once.

Cursing, he walked to the shower. His entire body instantly got onboard with the idea of seducing her. But though he knew that with a few kisses he could have her in his bed, he also knew the price for that kind of success was too high. Seducing her was no guarantee of keeping her in his life. What if they did have a brief time of happiness but in the end she left just as Laine had?

Worse… What if she stayed and lived her life miserable, deprived of any more children? She'd never have a little girl with her big brown eyes. Or another wild-haired baby boy.

Or even a son or daughter with her father's surgical skills and Sophie's kind heart.

Adoption was a solution but it was hollow. Yes, they'd have children to raise but they wouldn't be hers. They wouldn't be *theirs*. His circumstances demanded that any woman who wanted him in her life gave up the possibility of leaving her own legacy. Her own flesh and blood.

He knew the value of that. He'd found a way around it with his ranch. But a money legacy was one thing. The emotional connection of a mother and child was quite another. How could a woman in her twenties make such a dramatic choice?

She couldn't.

Not if she was smart.

When Jeb walked into the kitchen, Sophie didn't have to turn around to know it was him. All of her nerve endings went on red alert, as if they recognized his presence.

She knew he was upset and would probably revert to the cold, distant persona he'd used when she first arrived but she was determined not to let him. What he'd told her the night before flabbergasted her. In a sense, he'd forced her into the position of making *all* the decisions about their relationship after just two kisses. He'd basically said there was no point of a courtship, stolen kisses, moonlight walks, discussing possibilities. Unless she could tell him right now that she didn't want another child, he didn't want anything to do with her.

Well, she couldn't tell him that. What woman could? How could she say that loving him was worth giving up the possibility of ever being pregnant again, ever bearing another child, ever tickling the tummy of a being who had her genes?

She needed time, and not time spent tiptoeing around each other. They needed time interacting like normal people, getting to know each other, experimenting with what they felt in a normal way. And if it killed her she would take them back to the place they were yesterday. The teasing, fun, share-duties-with-Brady place where they could get to know each other enough that if decisions had to be made, they'd both have the knowledge to make them.

Ready to force him back to that place, she turned with a smile, but when she saw him, everything she wanted to say evaporated from her brain.

He stood in the doorway, a white towel wrapped around his neck, no shirt, no socks, only sweatpants clinging to his lean hips. His dark hair shone wetly from a recent shower. His gray-green eyes dark sparked with emotion.

Her breath stuttered in her chest. Wow.

What would it be like to wake up beside this handsome, sexy, passionate man every morning? Getting kisses every day that turned her blood to fire? Feeling his solid muscles curled around her as they drifted off to sleep?

He walked to the coffeemaker. "You and I need to talk about that kiss last night."

Not yet! She didn't want to discuss the night before. She didn't want him to tell her they should pretend nothing happened, pretend they didn't like or want each other. She wanted them to have time!

"That's not going to happen again."

"We're two people who are very attracted to each other. Common sense tells me that's going to happen a lot."

He turned from the counter. "It can't. I will never again commit to another woman. Especially not a woman who so obviously loves her child. Do you think I would deprive you of everything you truly need? Do you think I'm that selfish?"

She laughed. "Actually, yes, I do."

He gaped at her and she laughed again, knowing that if she tried to have this discussion in a serious way she'd probably tremble into oblivion. She had to be light and friendly in a pushy, honest way.

"How else do you explain cutting off the possibility of any relationship by forcing me to make a decision before I even know whether or not there should be a decision?"

"That's my point, Sophie. There shouldn't be a decision. I'm saving you the heartbreak of falling in love only to be disappointed."

She pulled a paper towel from the roll and cleaned up a spill by the sink. "How vain you are. You're so absolutely positive I'll fall in love that you won't even give me the options."

"Trust me. You don't want the options."

"How do you know?"

"I know."

"Because you hurt your ex-wife or because she hurt you?"

Taking a sip of coffee, he studied her over

the rim of his mug. Finally he said, "When you love somebody enough that's the same thing."

She stared at him in silence. Technically he'd just told her that he believed he could love *her* enough. This man who knew his mind, knew himself, knew what he wanted, was afraid of a relationship with her, not because he didn't think it would result in real love, but because he knew it would.

She turned to the counter again, wiped at the spot of the spill that she'd already cleaned. Now, she understood why he'd forced her into the position of making her choice the night before. He'd already made his. He might not be in love with her, but if they went any further, shared any more kisses, touched enough, he'd put himself in a danger zone. Unless she could say she accepted the fact that she'd have no more children, he knew he'd be hurt.

And she wasn't ready to make that choice.

So he was right. They couldn't take this any further.

He laughed emotionlessly, took another sip of his coffee and said, "Why don't we just say the whiskey made me kiss you last night and leave it at that?"

What a wonderful way out for two people in a situation so intense she could barely breathe. "Okay."

"And let's not be upset about this."

She blushed as guilt rattled through her. How could she be so cold to a man who deserved her warmth? Why couldn't she simply say she accepted that she'd never have another child? She had one. She'd had the experience of being pregnant, bearing him and nestling a newborn against her breast. Why couldn't she say one child was enough?

Because she'd had that child alone. Because that pregnancy hadn't been happy. It had been scary. Lonely. She'd made every discovery, experienced every "first" by herself. Not with the man she loved.

And that was the real bottom line. She didn't merely want another child. She wanted the experience of a pregnancy with a man who loved her. She wanted the whole package. She wanted him to buy her pickles and ice cream. She wanted to know what it felt like to have a husband holding her hand in labor. Telling her she was beautiful. Thanking her when it was over and he was holding a wailing newborn in his arms. His son. His progeny.

Still turned away from Jeb, she squeezed her eyes shut. Now she understood. As proud as Jeb was, he'd never feel right about depriving her of those things. He knew the depth of the loss she envisioned because it was his loss, too. He longed to thank somebody for giving him a child. He longed to hold a hand during labor. He might even yearn to be the one to buy pickles and ice cream, to satisfy cravings, to be a part of all those firsts.

Dear God. No wonder there was no argument for him. He knew what he was asking her to forfeit because he'd done it. And not out of choice. She couldn't push him or argue with him any more than she already had. That would only make him feel worse.

She feigned a smile and faced him. "All right. No fussing. No sulking."

He studied her a few seconds, undoubtedly recognizing her smile was forced, but at least her thoughts were clear. She agreed. They couldn't do this.

"So we're good? We both know anything romantic between us would be a mistake."

"Yes." All the emotion that had been riding

through her suddenly turned into a blank space, a feeling of emptiness so intense it stole her breath.

He picked up his travel mug and walked out of the kitchen, obviously on his way to his bedroom to dress for the day.

Sophie watched the door swing closed behind him.

She liked him.

He liked her.

And that emptiness she'd just felt wasn't her own. It was his. It had hurt him to deprive his ex-wife. He wouldn't be so cruel as to deprive her. But in protecting everybody else, he hurt himself.

Ironically that was part of why her attraction to him continually grew. He deserved love. Real love. Selfless, abiding, I'll-fight-for-you-forever love.

But she wasn't the woman to give it to him.

That afternoon Brady wouldn't take a nap. He fussed so much Sophie pulled him from the crib. "Is something wrong with you today, little buddy?"

He sniffed then rubbed his nose against her chest before starting to cry again.

Walking him to the kitchen, she hugged him tightly. "What's the matter?"

He only cried all the more.

"Are you sick?" She glanced down, as if she expected him to reply, and of course, he didn't. Remembering he'd gone through something similar when he'd gotten his first few teeth, she sat on a kitchen chair and rubbed her finger along his gums. On the bottom row she felt a bump. Remorse filled her. She hadn't immediately recognized his problem because she'd been preoccupied with Jeb's. Her guilt grew, as she realized yet another reason not to get involved in her boss's life. She had a baby who needed her.

"I'm sorry it took me so long to figure this out, but now that we're on the right page we'll be fine."

The door swung open and Jeb walked into the kitchen. "Everything okay?"

The air always left the room whenever Jeb entered and Sophie struggled for breath. Without even trying, he crackled with life and energy that translated into raw male sexuality. She couldn't imagine a woman loving him, knowing what it felt like to touch him and taste him, knowing what it felt like to be the object of his desire, and still leaving him. Though she understood his ex-wife's wish to have a child, she had a new set of doubts about the woman who had left Jeb. How could a woman love a man and desert him in *his* hour of need?

As she thought the last, Brady squirmed, as if Mother Nature was reminding her that her top priority wasn't her boss, but her son. She had to stop thinking about Jeb.

"He's getting a tooth."

"Poor little guy." He ran his fingers through Brady's downy hair sympathetically. "Do you have medicine or something to help him?"

She looked up, caught his gaze and swallowed hard at the emotion she saw in his eyes. In one day of interacting with her son, he already had strong feelings for her little boy. And she suddenly realized something that she should have seen before this. He didn't want her to keep Brady out from underfoot because he didn't want to be around her son. He'd wanted her to keep him away so he didn't grow attached to her child. He loved kids and didn't want to get attached to Brady only to have Sophie take him away when a better job came along, or she grew tired of ranch life…or she found love with someone else.

She looked away. There were so many ways she could hurt him. Was it any wonder he had been wary of her?

"I have gel for his gums. It numbs them enough that he can sleep. He's usually fine in a day or two."

"Then you go take care of him. I'll make my own supper."

"No. I'm—"

"No arguing. I realized today that you haven't taken a day off since you got here. Your boy needs tending. I can get my own supper."

"I know but—"

"No buts!" He put his hands on her shoulders and guided her to the door. "I'm fine."

The touch of his fingers on her shoulders made her close her eyes. Even a simple gesture shot sparks of fire through her.

She ignored them. Not because she didn't like Jeb, but because she did. Too much. And if she wasn't careful she'd sacrifice her dreams for a man she barely knew.

CHAPTER TEN

BRADY finally fell into a deep sleep around eight o'clock that night. Knowing he'd be good for several hours but not wanting to leave him, Sophie had settled on the sofa, pillow on her lap, ready to unwind by watching some television, when there was a knock at her door.

Confused, she sat up and set the pillow beside her. "Who is it?"

"It's me. Jeb."

She rolled her eyes, laughing at herself. Of course it was Jeb. Who else did she think it would be?

Shaking her head at her own stupidity, but forgiving herself since the past few hours with Brady had been difficult, she rose from the sofa and opened her door.

"Sorry." She smiled sheepishly. "It's been a hellish few hours."

He produced two brown bottles of beer from behind his back. "I sort of figured, so I brought you a beer."

Surprised, she smiled at him. "Thanks."

"I also need to talk with you about a few things."

"Oh?" The tone in his voice sent shivers of fear through her. He was a very observant man, and busy as she had been with Brady, she hadn't been careful about her reactions to him that day. What if he'd figured out the conclusions she'd been drawing by the expressions on her face? What if it embarrassed him to realize she had been thinking about him, about his life, about what he'd gone through?

She opened the door a little wider. "Come in."

He stepped into the room, handed her one of the bottles and took a seat on the chair, which seemed to disappear around him.

Laughing, she sat on the sofa. "Chair's a little small."

He frowned down at it. "Not very comfortable, either."

Knowing they could chitchat all night when she'd rather get this over with, she said, "What did you need to talk about?"

"I got two phone calls this evening."

"One from Slim I'm hoping."

He took a swig of beer. "Yep. If his older sister can't handle caring for their mom, he's out for the summer."

He said it in such a somber way that Sophie's spirits lifted. Maybe his guarded mood wasn't the result of her making him feel bad about himself, but worry over running the ranch and his business without Slim.

"That's awful."

"We can manage. Especially since the other call was from the clients. They've canceled their visit."

"Oh, no! Do you have any *good* news?"

He chuckled, leaning back in the chair, looking casual and sexy and totally unconcerned, almost as if he functioned best when others needed him to be strong.

"It gives us more time to get ready for them."

"So, they're still coming?"

"Yep."

"How long do we have?"

Jeb shrugged. "Mrs. Baker said they just need a week or two. Mr. Baker's current picture ran over and he can't get away from the set."

Sophie's eyes widened. "He's a movie star?"

"Director."

"Oh."

"Don't be disappointed. Directors are important, too."

"I know. I was just kind of hoping to meet somebody cool."

"Oh, trust me. He's cool. He wears sunglasses in the house."

She laughed and took her first swig of beer. "I can't drink this whole thing."

"You're a lightweight?"

His horrified expression caused a giggle to bubble from her. "No. I can hold my own. I simply can't get tipsy tonight. I'll probably have to get up with Brady."

"He won't sleep through the night?"

"Not when he's teething."

"I'd take part of the watch for you, but that means I'd have to sleep on that." He pointed at the square sofa. "I don't think that's a good idea for my back."

She glanced down at her beer. Just as she'd suspected, he was such a natural with kids that he didn't think before he volunteered. If Brady was around, he'd be involved. If she didn't keep to the rules he'd set, he'd be the one to be hurt.

"I can handle it, but thanks for offering."

"Why are you always so surprised when somebody does something nice for you?"

"I'm not. I expected you to offer to help. What surprises me is that you don't realize how nice you are."

He burst out laughing. "You need to have a conversation with my last housekeeper. She'd totally disagree with you."

She took a drink of her beer. "Right. I'm guessing she's the reason you don't realize you're nice."

"Stop saying I'm nice. I'm not."

She winced. "That's right. I forgot men don't like to be thought of as nice."

He scowled. "Now you're making fun of me."

"Sort of. But you can't deny that you're worried about Brady, or that you pay well— or even that you treat your ranch foreman like a brother."

"I threatened to fire Slim for teasing me the day you asked if you could take a walk around the ranch."

"Yet he still orchestrated the two of us going out on a ride." She smiled. "And when his mom got sick you lent him your private plane. Without a second thought."

His scowl deepened. "I'm not nice."

"Again, you're not going to get *me* to believe that." She motioned around the room. She might not be the woman to love him, but that didn't mean she couldn't make her mark on his life. And her best way would be to get him over the hurdle of thinking he didn't deserve to be loved. He did.

"This place is a hundred times better than what I could afford on my own," she said, ticking off the things he'd already done for her. "You're keeping me on, when you could have stuck to our three-week deal, because you know how much this job means to me. If I stay long enough, you'd eventually treat Brady like a son."

She stopped, suddenly realizing what she'd said.

Silence cloaked the room in oppression.

He took a long drink that drained his beer bottle, and then very quietly said, "We both know that's not a good idea." He rose. "I'll see you in the morning."

Filled with remorse for not thinking through her stupid, offhand remark, she rose, too. "Okay."

He headed for the door, but suddenly faced

her. "And I'm not nice." With slow, deliberate steps, he closed the distance between them. "Given half a chance, I'd ravish you. I'd kiss you until you couldn't breathe for wanting me and then I'd take my time making love to you. I wouldn't think about tomorrow, consequences be damned." He slid his palm to her cheek, his thumb caressing it softly, seductively. "You'd be in my bed, simply because I want you and some days I can't control that."

She looked away, and he lifted her chin until she caught his gaze. "Think about that the next time you're tempted to believe I'm nice."

With that he kissed her. Dumbfounded by the raw need in his voice and the truth in his words, she hadn't steeled herself for the touch of his mouth against hers. When their lips met, she simply melted, fell into the sinful sensations, opened to him, accepted the rub of his tongue as it swept into her mouth.

Heat poured through her, causing her stomach to clench and her breasts to expand with life and need. Of its own volition, her body pressed against his, finding the hard evidence of his desire. Her hands skimmed the strong arms holding her, until they reached his broad shoulders, his neck, and slid into his thick, silky hair.

He pulled away, brushing his lips from her mouth to her chin, down her neck to the sensitive crevice there. Running them along her collarbone, he quietly said, "I won't tie you to me when I can't give you what you need. But unless you can tell me that it's okay for us to make love—even if it's only once—you're going to have to be strong enough for both of us."

The strength he spoke of eluded her, but he stepped away. "Don't settle for less than what you want. Not even for me."

The next morning the air sizzled when Jeb walked into the kitchen. The kiss the night before told her exactly how much he wanted her, and reminded her of exactly how much she wanted him. He hadn't spoken of love. Hadn't made excuses or proposed alternatives for not being able to have children. He'd warned her away from him, even as he told her he didn't intend to resist her.

When their eyes met, the sizzle that had entered the room with him increased exponentially. Her pulse scrambled. Her chest tightened. Her blood burst into flame.

Just from a look.

What would happen if they ever did make love?

"Good morning."

She cleared her throat. "Good morning."

"How's Brady?"

"He was awake most of the night, so now he's sleeping like a lamb. He probably won't be up before noon."

A hush fell over the room, and she realized what she'd said. Her baby was tended. Jeb had given the hands a much-needed day off due to the client's cancellation. Slim was in Texas. They were alone in the big quiet house. And they burned for each other.

She quickly turned to the sink, shoved her hands in the dishwater and picked up a glass.

Without a word, he stepped behind her, pushed the hair from her neck and brushed a kiss across her nape. She squeezed her eyes shut, reveling in the sensation, knowing that one of these days she would succumb, not sure at this moment if he was warning her— or seducing her—and terrified that she didn't have the will to resist.

"Lucy, I'm home!"

Slim's voice rang through the downstairs and Sophie started, but Jeb slowly pulled away. His lips rose from her nape, leaving a cool sensation in their wake. His hands slid from her waist. He stepped back, away from her, just as Slim pushed open the swinging door.

Dressed in jeans and a lightweight plaid shirt, he walked toward the table and picked up the conversation as if he hadn't been away. "I hear you have news."

Jeb walked to the coffeemaker. "Clients canceled," he said simply, his voice gruff with sexual need that Sophie prayed Slim wouldn't notice.

"Monty wasn't clear," Slim said, appearing blissfully ignorant. "He wasn't sure if they weren't coming at all or if they'd just postponed."

"Postponed." Jeb turned from the coffeemaker, pot in hand. "Want some?"

"Sure. You got any pie?"

"Yes." Sophie heard the squeak in her own voice and winced. She cleared her throat. "How's your mom?"

"Good. Once she's out of the hospital, she's moving in with my older sister, but only for a month or so. She's adamant about going back home."

"So your sister could take her in?"

"She set up a bedroom in her den, near a downstairs bathroom." Slim took a swig of coffee. "So they're all set."

"That's good," Jeb and Sophie said in unison and though Jeb didn't seem to think anything of it, Sophie realized they were growing so close they were beginning to talk alike. Jeb might be able to compartmentalize his feelings for her and keep them purely sexual, but what she felt for him was personal, intimate, a real connection.

She suddenly understood what he'd been telling her all along. Too much time in each other's company and they would be in love. And then the choices would be snatched from her. Starry-eyed from intimacy and a life-changing connection, she'd downplay the fact that loving him meant giving up everything else. She wouldn't consider how she'd feel twenty years from now when she had only one child to walk down the aisle. Only one child to give her grandchildren. Only one child.

* * *

Jeb spent the rest of the day following Slim, telling himself he was getting his foreman reoriented, but he was really avoiding private time with Sophie and her son. He knew what he wanted. The woman *and* her little boy. The ready-made family. He also knew the kind of man he was. Strong. Determined. Not one to take no for an answer. If he pulled out all the stops, he'd win. He always did. And then what would happen? Ten years, five years...maybe even two years from now, she'd wake up one morning realizing she'd forfeited her dreams and she'd hate him.

In the end he really wouldn't win. And he'd hurt her. Maybe even Brady. If she left after Brady and Jeb had bonded, the little boy would see him as the dad he longed to be and they'd both scream in pain at the loss.

So he stayed away. Out of sight. Out of mind. Hoping to take things back to normal.

But as the day wore on, he suddenly remembered that Sophie now made his dinner. Knowing any private time with her would take them back to the place neither one of them wanted to be, he called Slim to the barn office.

"While you were gone, Sophie and I had some conversations."

Slim fell to the seat in front of the desk. "Oh, yeah?"

Jeb picked up a pencil and tapped it on his desk blotter. "Yeah. I was so busy she started making my dinner and before we knew it, I sort of got accustomed to Brady."

"Hey, that's great!"

"Yeah. Once we realized Brady wasn't a problem for me anymore, I couldn't see any reason she couldn't stay... So she's permanent now."

Slim's eyes widened. "What else happened while I was away?"

Not about to touch that with a ten-foot pole, Jeb pretended great interest in his phone messages, leafing through them, avoiding Slim's gaze. "Nothing, except now that I've got dinner on her agenda again, it might be a good idea for you to eat with me so we can debrief at the end of the day."

Slim laughed. "Are you asking me to supper?"

Jeb scowled. "It's not a date."

"If her dinners are as good as her cookies and pie I'm still in."

They walked to the house discussing the ranch. When they entered the kitchen, Sophie turned from the stove.

Her gaze moved from Jeb to Slim and she smiled with relief. "Hey, are you eating here tonight?"

"Yep." Slim rubbed his hands together in anticipation. He sniffed the air. "Pot roast." He sniffed again. "And mashed potatoes."

Sophie laughed. "You're good."

"Nope, just hungry." He ambled to the table. "Hey, Brady."

The baby cooed.

Jeb also took his regular seat. "Hey, Brady."

Sophie scrambled to the table with another plate and silverware. "I'll be ready in a second."

Seeing she'd only brought enough utensils for him, Slim frowned. "You're not eating with us—"

"I—"

"She—"

Sophie scurried back to the stove. Slim peered at Jeb. "What's this all about? She'll have to clean up twice if she waits to eat until after we're done." He glanced at Sophie, then back to Jeb. "You don't have a problem with her eating with us, do you, boss?"

Knowing he'd sound like an idiot if he admitted that he did, Jeb said, "No. Especially if it means less work for her." He twisted in his chair to address Sophie. "Come eat with us."

She nodded, but she wouldn't look at him.

Jeb turned back to Slim. Sophie set her place then brought the food to the table. Slim grabbed a healthy helping of pot roast and between bites began asking questions about what had happened with the hands while he was gone.

Within seconds the awkwardness had passed, Jeb caught Sophie's gaze. She smiled hopefully. He took a breath then looked away. They could do this.

CHAPTER ELEVEN

TWO FRIDAYS LATER, Jeb awakened out of sorts. Grumpy. Groggy. Even after a steamy shower, he ambled to the kitchen feeling something like a bear with a thorn in its paw.

As always, Brady sat in his high chair. Sophie stood at the counter, fixing the baby's breakfast. Something stirred in Jeb's psyche, but before it rose enough that he could label it longing for what he couldn't have, he squelched it.

The little boy screeched at him.

"Hey, kid."

Sophie brought the cereal to the table. "He's in a rare mood today. Watch yourself."

Jeb laughed. "You think he's in a rare mood?" He grabbed one of the regular mugs from the cupboard, filled it with coffee and walked to the table. "He's got nothing on me today."

"Oh, yeah?" she asked, sliding a spoon of cereal into Brady's open mouth. "What's up?"

He could have told her that he wanted to sleep with her so much that some nights he actually plotted strategies to sneak into her room. He could have told her that he resented the easy way she fit into his life as a maid when he really wanted her for a lover. He could have said he resented the way she made him feel comfortable and edgy at the same time. Or that it made him mad that he could see she needed a job more than he needed to sleep with her.

Instead he said, "I have no idea," but something tripped in his brain. A memory that wouldn't quite form.

Something *was* nagging at him. And for once it was something more than wanting to sleep with her. He just couldn't put his finger on it.

"I have this weird feeling that I've forgotten something."

Silence descended as Sophie aimed a spoon of cereal at Brady's mouth and Jeb took a sip of coffee.

Slim entered the kitchen through the back door. Sophie said, "There are cookies. Oatmeal. Just out of the oven."

Jeb fought the urge to squeeze his eyes

shut. Did she have to be so sweet? If she were a tad more selfish, or inconsiderate, or even a bit grouchy he could probably sleep with her simply for sex. Instead with someone nice like her, emotion had gotten involved and it shook an angry finger at him every time he even casually considered seducing her.

Slim headed for the cookie jar. "Great. I skipped breakfast."

Jeb turned in his chair and faced Slim. "So what's on the agenda today?"

"Nothing for you. I've got a handle on it. You can go about your business as usual."

"With the Baker postponement I'm sort of at loose ends."

Slim shoved a cookie into his mouth and headed for the door. "Not my problem."

As the door closed behind Slim, Jeb turned to Sophie. "What are you doing today?"

Sophie paused in feeding her son and he pounded on the tray, screeching angrily. She sighed. "Whatever I'm doing, I'll be doing it with Brady on my arm."

He glanced at the baby, then back at Sophie and knew the real reason he wouldn't seduce her into something she didn't want. She had a baby, responsibilities. His natural inclination would be to ask how he could help, but he knew that wouldn't be wise. He couldn't fall into the role of her baby's daddy, no matter how much he wanted it. And some days he resented that.

He pulled in a breath. He *was* in a mood.

"But it doesn't matter. With the extra time we've had," Sophie said, still feeding Brady. "Even I'm down to putzing around. To tell you the truth I'm kind of getting bored."

"Yeah, me, too." He rose from the table and grabbed his coffee. "I'm going to check my emails."

He left the kitchen and strolled back to the office, wishing he could get rid of this feeling. But he couldn't. He tried to remind himself that he and Sophie were wrong for each other. They were different, had different needs, wanted different things, so he shouldn't like her. But he did. And he paid for it. Every damned day she and her baby sat at the tips of his fingers, as if fate were taunting him with everything he wanted but couldn't have.

His life sucked.

At his desk, he grabbed the calendar, flopped into the tall-back chair, lowered his gaze to that day's entries and forgot all about being angry and moody.

Today was the day of the groundbreaking for Samuel's House. Not only did he have to be a hundred miles away in less than three hours, but he also had to write a speech.

Damn.

That's why he'd forgotten. He hated speeches, so he'd pushed the whole event to the back of his mind, hoping it would go away. But it wouldn't. It was here. And he had to say a few words on behalf of his parents as well as himself. There was no way out.

He bounced out of his chair as if his butt were on fire and ran into the kitchen. "Call Slim, have him call the pilot and tell him I've got to be in the air in an hour."

She turned from the sink. "In the air? I guess this must be the thing you forgot? Where are you going?"

Good grief. Had he ever met a woman so curious, or one who had such a clever way of getting him to talk about himself—

He stopped his ranting because he'd hit a relevant truth. She *could* get him to talk. She pulled things out of him no one else had ever been able to.

"You haven't done any writing by any chance, have you?"

"Writing?"

"I need a speech."

"A speech? Whatever for? Does this have something to do with Samuel's House?" She winced. "Working at your desk I found the files."

"Then you'll know I'm a sponsor. Today is the groundbreaking for a new facility and I'm supposed to say something."

"Just speak from the heart."

"Yeah, right. I'll get up in front of a hundred people and say 'uh' about fifty times." He gave her his best pleading look. After the sleepless nights he'd endured because of her, she owed him. "Come on. Fly along. Help me think of something to say."

He'd sounded so desperate and the invitation had sounded so innocent that Sophie had forgotten how powerful their attraction was and she'd agreed.

She felt the first wave of reminder when he walked down the stairs to the foyer. Wearing boots, black jeans and a white shirt with a bolero tie, he looked sexily Western. Everything female in her responded.

And she was going to spend an entire day with him?

Without stuttering or falling into his arms?

Fastening his watch on his wrist, he said, "You ready?"

She peered down at her simple sundress and sandals, then took another look at him. He was the epitome of a rich rancher. She looked like a surfer girl.

Maybe she didn't have anything to worry about?

"Yeah, I'm ready."

Finally done with his watch, he glanced at her. "Wow."

Then he saw Brady sitting in the travel seat beside her. His expression changed from normal man gazing hungrily at a woman he found attractive, to normal man looking at a baby.

And everything fell into place again.

He'd never act on his attraction to her, not even in a teasing kind of way because of Brady. He didn't mind having her baby around, but he also didn't want to grow too fond of him, too attached to him, too close to him, because he didn't want to end up hurt. Or Brady to end up hurt. Or her to end up hurt.

He'd thought it all through and acted out his conclusion by not ever mentioning his feelings for her. If he even still had them. It had been so long since they'd been alone or talked, he might have grown immune to her.

She had nothing to fear.

"The kid's coming?"

"Is that okay?"

He shrugged. "Doesn't matter to me. Let's go."

They got into an SUV and drove to a landing strip on the ranch. Stepping into a plane that looked more like a living room, she just barely held back her gasp of awe. At the back was a bar. Silky drapes decorated the windows. Her feet sunk into thick carpeting. Two rows of buttery-brown leather seats sat across from each other.

She walked to one side. Jeb walked to the other. After settling Brady in the baby seat, she buckled herself in.

Jeb pushed a button that activated an intercom system. With a word to the cockpit, the plane began to move. It didn't take them long to get into the air. Once they were cruising, Jeb removed his seat belt. "Anything you want? A sandwich? A drink?"

"No, I'm fine."

"Then let's get started." He pushed a button that caused a little table to slide out from the wall beside him then pulled a few note cards from his jacket pocket. "I guess I'll start off with good afternoon."

She laughed. "Makes sense. Then thank everybody for their hard work. Somebody somewhere did something to get this thing going... Even if you don't know who or what, so thanking everybody will cover it."

He nodded. "Okay. That's good. Then what?"

"Well, if it were me, I'd just say what I feel about the building. What does this project mean to you?"

He took a breath. "A lot."

She leaned her elbow on the arm of her seat, and put her chin on her closed fist. "Really? How'd you get involved with an orphanage anyway?"

"It's not an orphanage. It's a transitional care facility."

She frowned. "What's a transitional care facility?"

"It's a place where kids who can't make it in foster care go."

"Oh, hard cases. So how'd you get involved with something like that?"

"I caught a kid—Billy Clark—stealing a few years back, and by the time I drove him into town to the sheriff, I'd bonded with him. Parents were drug addicts. He was stealing to feed his sister."

"That's awful!"

"Yeah, well, I thought so, too, and I didn't press charges. But we sent social services out to their house. Billy and his sister were to go into foster care and though his sister easily adapted, Billy couldn't. He ran away and ran away and ran away until—"

He stopped. Sophie reached across the aisle and touched his forearm. "Until what?"

"Until he fell in with the wrong crowd and was involved in an armed robbery where a man was killed. He's now in a state facility, probably for life."

"I'm sorry."

"Not half as sorry as I was. I thought I'd failed him. He wasn't my responsibility but he had no one else and somehow I just kept missing the mark—probably because at the time I didn't have much real world training. My upbringing hadn't prepared me for anybody like him and I didn't know what to say to him. I didn't know the signs that he was in trouble. I was such an airhead." He shook his head in dismay. "Anyway, my parents visited me about a week after his sentencing, and their cavalier attitude about life infuriated me. I exploded and we got into a fight and before I knew it I was telling them they needed to do something about Billy...or at the very least kids like Billy." He smiled. "Imagine my surprise when they did."

"So your parents aren't as bad as you thought?"

"They're still beach bums." He paused to laugh and Sophie could see that he and his parents might have different goals and ideals, but they loved each other. "They could see I was serious about starting this facility and they put up some cash, too."

"And you keep up with it?"

"Hey, it's a good cause and something worthwhile for my parents to spend their money on. I'm happy to throw in a few bucks and make a few trips."

"You just don't like speeches."

He rolled his eyes. "Who does?"

"Good point. Okay, so once you thank everybody, just talk about the service you believe the facility provides for the community. Say you and your parents are proud to be involved with it." She smiled. "Then sit down."

He laughed. "That part I can handle."

"I don't know why you're so nervous."

"I don't like speaking to groups. I'm much better one-on-one. And when there's no emotion involved." He caught her gaze. "I hate this emotion junk."

"No kidding." But she smiled. He really had a heart of gold. Which was really why he hated speeches. No man wanted to look soft and vulnerable. Especially not with the media watching.

But that was also why he didn't want to get too close to Brady. He knew the little boy would pull him in and make him feel like a father, and when Sophie left he'd be lonelier than if he'd never experienced what it would be like to be a daddy.

They finished the speech and then Sophie closed her eyes, not forcing him into any more discussions. She respected his feelings and he respected hers. There was no point belaboring the issue.

Slim had called ahead and made arrangements for a car to be waiting for them at the airport. They drove a short distance to the building site and, within minutes, Sophie was being introduced to a long line of people.

Every person, from the lowliest social worker to the tycoons who made up the board of directors for the facility, grinned at her. From their comments it was easy to see this was the first time Jeb had ever brought a woman to one of their events, and most of them believed they were romantically involved.

She wanted to say, "Nice to meet you but I'm Jeb's housekeeper." Instead, not wanting to cause a stir, she only said, "Nice to meet you."

The ceremony began, Jeb said his few words after Pete Malloy, executive director of Samuel's House, gave a long speech. Shovels angled into the dirt, Jeb, Pete Malloy and the executive board posed for pictures.

Sophie smiled, her heart turning over in her chest. She knew how much he hated this, yet he did it anyway. Not because he was good but because he was wonderful. Selfless. Generous.

She let her gaze ripple across the crowd and

back to him. So many people depended on him. Including her. Yet, he didn't brag. He quietly did what he perceived needed to be done.

Pete Malloy hustled over to Sophie, beating Jeb by two seconds. "We're serving cookies and punch, if you're interested."

Jeb said, "Maybe another time," at the same time that Sophie said, "I'd love a cookie."

Pete said, "Great! Just follow my SUV."

When he walked away, Sophie winced. "Sorry."

"That's okay. Neither one of us had anything to do today anyway."

They made their way to the existing Samuel's House facility, which was only around the bend from the open field where the new building was to be built. Sophie got out of the SUV and unbuckled Brady who was waking up from the long sleep he'd drifted into listening to Pete Malloy's speech.

"Hey, buddy," she crooned as she lifted him out of his seat.

Jeb came around to her side of the car. "Want me to take the carrier in for you?"

His question surprised her. But then she wondered why. True, he might not carry the little boy around on his shoulder, but he'd folded her and Brady into his life so naturally that the three of them lived together comfortably.

Like a family.

She shook her head to dislodge that thought. That was crazy. "No. I think I'll hold him."

They walked into the building that was nothing like Sophie expected. The furniture appeared to be new and though magazines and books littered the end tables of the main room, the fresh scent of cleaning solutions greeted them.

"Wow. This house is great! Why did you think you needed a new one?"

Jeb put his hand on the small of her back and directed her back down the hall to a dining room. From the easy movement, Sophie suspected he didn't even realize what he was doing, but Sophie did. He was so casual with her that he really did treat her like family. Not a housekeeper. He wasn't trying to make them fit. He didn't have to. He was so accustomed to her and Brady, that he was now adding them into this part of his world.

"We're building a new place because this house is no longer big enough." He glanced around, pulled in a breath and faced her.

"There are thousands of kids out there who need us. We'll never even know about most of them. But I want to have room for everybody we find."

His serious expression caused Sophie's heart to melt. He genuinely cared about these kids. He was such a good man that it was hard not to like him. But he'd proven himself to be a good person long before this. She'd even grown to like him long before this. And that was the problem. Seeing this side of him, she was falling over the edge. Up to this point they'd both managed to stop short of that one little word that could cause so much trouble. But here she stood, face-to-face with his generosity, his commitment, and it was simply too much.

Unless she got a hold of herself, before this trip was over she'd be head over heels in love.

They entered a room filled with a combination of adults and teenagers, all of whom seemed to know Jeb.

"Hey, Mr. Worthington."

"Hey, Aaron." Jeb offered his hand for shaking. "How've you been?"

"Good. Gonna graduate next spring."

"I told you that if you stayed it would be worth it."

"Yeah, we'll see. When I can't get anything but a fast food job, I'm coming to you."

"No, you're going to college."

"Right."

"The funds are already in place."

"Yeah, for tuition. Where am I gonna live? On the street?"

"We'll work something out."

Sophie pulled in a breath. He was so good with these kids. It amazed her that he'd ever believed he wasn't cut out to be a dad. But more than that, it amazed her that she'd ever been able to resist him. She was no longer worried that she'd fall in love with him because it was too late. She was already in love.

And that was going to be trouble.

As more teenagers gathered around him, Sophie got pushed to the side. Pete Malloy strolled up to her. Pointing to Jeb with his punch glass he said, "He's quite an interesting man, isn't he? There's never a dull moment when he visits."

The urge to tell Pete that he didn't know the half of it bubbled up inside her. Instead she turned to the Samuel's House director with a smile. "You should try living with him."

"So you're living together?"

Sophie winced. If nothing else, she had to nip that rumor in the bud right now. "I'm his maid."

"Oh." The embarrassed expression on Pete's face was priceless. "I'm so sorry."

"Don't be." Not only had he clued her in that she was probably looking at Jeb with stars in her eyes, but also Pete had given her the opportunity to dispel the rumor before it caught fire and couldn't be pulled back.

More than that, he'd reminded her of her real place in Jeb's life. His maid. He might be interesting enough, kind enough, generous enough that she'd fallen in love with him. But she was his employee. A single woman with a child who'd desperately needed a job. A woman who sassed him. And who'd been stunned speechless when he'd told her his biggest secret, that he couldn't have kids. She hadn't been supportive. She'd frozen.

How could he possibly like a woman who'd thought of herself first, not him. Even the memory of that night shamed her.

"We've obviously crossed the line from boss and employee into friendship. So it's not a big deal."

"I can see how that could happen."

She followed Pete's gaze to Jeb and her

heart ached. How she must have hurt him by her silence. It was no wonder he'd stopped any possibility of a relationship between them. Here he was, a man who didn't care about biology, who cared for dozens of children. Why would he attach himself to a woman whose heart didn't expand any further than herself?

"He's a genuinely nice guy. Bit of a curiosity, though. If I spent any more time with him, I'd probably be poking into his life. Trying to get the inside scoop."

Sophie laughed. "Trust me. You wouldn't get it."

"Close mouthed?"

"Extremely."

"Too bad. I'd love to know what happened in the Zoe situation."

"The Zoe situation?"

"Yeah. Zoe's a little girl Jeb and his ex had considered adopting."

Her eyes widened. "Oh?"

Pete nodded. "She was the youngest kid we'd ever had come here and she clearly didn't fit. Jeb and Laine developed a soft spot for her and the next thing you know the word adoption had come up. Then out of nowhere her mom appeared—clean and sober—with a job and an apartment. She took Zoe and from all accounts everything worked out."

Sophie said nothing. She wasn't amazed that Jeb would consider adopting a child. She'd seen his commitment to this place, these kids. What surprised her was that she'd had no clue.

"Everything ended well for Zoe...but the next event we had, Jeb arrived as a divorced man."

Sophie's mouth fell open. She told herself not to pry, but she couldn't stop herself. "You think losing the child had something to do with Jeb's divorce?"

"Yes."

Jeb ambled over. "Are you telling her all my secrets?"

Pete had the good graces to look embarrassed. "Just the ones I know."

"Then I'm glad I never really told you anything." He faced Sophie. "Pete and I need a minute with the board of directors. Do you mind?"

She shook her head, looking at Jeb with a whole new perspective. He'd been told he couldn't have kids, then the one child he'd wanted to adopt had been snatched from him. It was no wonder he believed he'd never be a father. "No. Go on. I'll be fine."

"Great." He motioned for Pete to walk with him. "There are apparently some papers we need to sign."

"Okay," Pete said as they disappeared into the milling crowd.

"You Jeb's woman?"

Sophie turned at the question to see a young man looking at her curiously.

"I'm his maid."

"No kidding! He's got a maid?"

She laughed. "Yep."

"Hey, Jordie!" the kid called, motioning to a tall, slender boy to join them. "This here's Worthington's maid."

The boy walked over. "You're a maid?"

Hoisting Brady a little higher on her arm, Sophie said, "Yes."

"I'll bet he lives in a big old mansion."

"It's more of a house…" She stopped as two more kids joined them. Both girls. Both around fifteen. Both wearing too much eye makeup. One with a ring in her nose.

"Does he have a dog?"

"Horses."

A general affirmative sound rose from the group, as three more kids walked over.

"He's got a ranch, right?"

The question came from somewhere in the growing crowd and Sophie hesitated. She'd always known Jeb was a private person, but the few things she'd heard from Pete today magnified just how much he held to his privacy. He wouldn't want her talking about him and she didn't want to endanger his confidence in her. The only thing she could think to do to get the conversation away from him was to turn the tables.

"Yes, he has a ranch." She smiled at the first kid. "So what's your name?"

"Orlando. This here's Jordie. That's Mark and Austin," He said pointing to the two boys to his right. "That's Birdie and Macayla's the one with the nose ring."

Sophie smiled at each one. "It's nice to meet you."

"Where are you from?"

Sophie should have realized she was no match for the questions of a group of curious kids, but at least the questions were no longer about Jeb. "California."

"California?" The girls gasped.

Orlando was much too cool for that. He nodded. "The big C."

"Yep."

They managed to fire off enough questions to fill the entire space of time that Jeb and Pete were gone. Though they laughed a lot, Sophie's gaze continually drifted to Macayla. The girl needed somebody. She didn't have to say the words. Her confused eyes told the story. They also told the story of why Jeb and his ex-wife had considered adopting one of the children who lived at Samuel's House. The boys and even Birdie had a maturity about them that didn't match their ages, but an innocent like Macayla stuck out like a sore thumb. If someone didn't catch her now, God only knew where she'd land when she fell.

Jeb strode over with a groan. "Are they grilling you about me?"

She laughed. "They tried, but I managed to change the subject."

"Great. Let's go."

The kids protested, but Jeb promised a return visit soon. Again, it was easy for Sophie to see that the kids admired him, loved his visits and trusted that he would take care of them.

They said goodbye and headed for the door. Though all of the boys and even Birdie disbursed casually, Macayla stayed where she was. She didn't speak. Didn't move. Simply watched Sophie and Jeb leave.

At the door, Sophie turned one final time. Her gaze caught Macayla's and she had the sudden, intense intuition that *she* was the person created to mother this child.

CHAPTER TWELVE

AFTER Jeb confirmed with the pilot that he and Sophie were settled in, ready to take off, he leaned back in his chair and feigned sleep. But after only a few seconds, he opened his eyes.

"I know what you're thinking."

"How could you possibly know what I'm thinking?"

"Because I thought the same things myself."

She laughed. "Right. So what am I thinking?"

"That that little girl needs a home."

She caught his gaze across the aisle of the plane. She blinked once, twice, but she didn't refute what he'd said.

"You need to remember that these kids are street kids. The kind of home you'd make for somebody like Macayla would stifle her."

"Or be exactly what she needs."

He shook his head. "What she needs is to

learn how to live in a normal environment, to pull her weight in chores to earn her place. The last thing she wants to be is beholden to someone."

"And you know this because?"

"Because I read every file."

"You do?"

He nearly growled at his mistake. How was it that this woman could get him to tell her things he never told anyone? "Yes." He sucked in an annoyed breath. "Don't make me out to be a saint."

But he saw from the glimmer that came to her eyes that that was exactly what she'd done.

"I know you're not a saint, but I also see you don't give yourself credit for the good things you do."

"I give a few speeches, read a few files. If you want to direct those stars in your eyes at somebody, go look at my parents. They're the ones who put up the money."

But the spark stayed in her eyes and it killed him. He wanted to be everything she saw. But he wasn't good. He was flawed. And he'd best not forget that.

* * *

Sophie made a simple supper of macaroni and cheese and fried fish, still feeling the push of maternal instincts for Macayla that was as sharp and keen as what she felt when she first held Brady. Though Jeb didn't mention Samuel's House or their trip that afternoon and kept his focus on the discussion he was having with Slim, Sophie couldn't shake the thoughts of Macayla. She hadn't felt anything like this when she looked at Orlando or any of the other kids at Samuel's House. And for that reason alone, she didn't want to ignore it.

After Brady fell asleep, she went to Jeb's office and found the Samuel's House file. She retrieved Pete Malloy's email address, wrote an email asking if Macayla had an email address and sent it across cyberspace. To her surprise, Pete replied within a few seconds. Though he encouraged her to make friends with Macayla, he also set ground rules for Sophie, telling her to keep the emails light and friendly and not to play psychologist or stand-in parent. He reminded her that she wasn't a therapist and that there were trained staff members to handle Macayla's big problems.

Doing exactly as Pete suggested, she wrote an email simply telling Macayla it was nice to meet her and hit Send, knowing it was up to Macayla whether or not they'd become friends.

When Jeb didn't arrive in the kitchen for coffee on Sunday morning, Sophie suspected he was avoiding her. She confirmed that suspicion on Monday when she walked into the kitchen to find a pot of coffee had already been brewed and at least two cups taken, but Jeb was nowhere in sight. By Wednesday, having only seen him at meals with Slim, she knew the trip to Samuel's House, or maybe her reaction to it, had caused him to decide to keep his distance.

Which was fine, maybe even for the best. She hadn't meant to fall in love with him, but she had and now she had to figure out what to do about it. Her head told her to do nothing and given the way he was avoiding her, Sophie realized that was probably the right thing to do. The feelings she had for him were new. Fragile. She didn't think they would go away. But she also wasn't sure what she should do about them. Did she dare tell him and risk rejection? But if she didn't tell him, could she live with a man she loved, cook for him, clean for him…and never have his love in return?

After tidying the kitchen and putting Brady into bed for a nap she went to the office to check her email. Macayla had answered.

She let a day go by before answering Macayla, if only because she didn't want to put any pressure on her, and life fell into a casual routine with Sophie spending most of her time alone with Brady, keeping up the house and planning meals. She typically served Jeb and Slim lunch, then sat down and ate supper with them. The conversation didn't turn to her often. Typically the meal was spent listening to Slim give a report of what had happened at the ranch that day.

Both Jeb and Slim always thanked her for meals. But her part of the conversation rarely extended beyond that and she soon realized that things were actually working out. She and Jeb could live in the same house, and she didn't have to worry that her feelings for him would cause her to do something that would ruin her stay at the ranch.

So it surprised her when Jeb returned to the kitchen on Thursday night just as she was finishing up the dishes.

For the first time in weeks, they were alone. Everything she'd felt for him at the groundbreaking for Samuel's House came tumbling back. He was good, kind, generous. Sexy, sweet and funny. How could a woman see that and not love him?

Their gazes met, but Jeb quickly looked away.

And Sophie forced herself back to reality. She might love him. He might have feelings for her. But he also had issues and she needed this job. She had to respect that.

He walked to the table. "Can you give me a minute?"

She said, "Sure," but something about his ominous tone caused her tummy to tingle. She swore she hadn't treated him any differently since she realized she loved him, but what if she had? What if he guessed or sensed that her feelings had changed? What if he couldn't work with her knowing how she felt?

He took a seat at the round table and Sophie sat across from him.

He slid an envelope from his pocket. "As you know, the ranch management company direct deposits your salary into your checking account."

Her heart stopped. "It's payday?"

He laughed. "Yes. Finally. We hold back two weeks pay and only pay once a month, so you probably thought you'd never see cash. But here's your paystub."

"Oh!" Joy coursed through her. She'd been dying to see money appear in her checking account like magic, and here it was!

"I want you to open that now because the money's a bit more than you expected."

She glanced up at him. His eyes were soft and serious. He worried about her reaction.

"The first month, you weren't just doing maid's work—you were also decorating. So I had my accountant check into average salaries for decorators and that's reflected in your deposit."

She looked down at the amount that had gone into her checking account. Her mouth fell open. "Holy cow."

He laughed. "The decorating you did was worth every penny."

She swallowed. The extra he'd paid her would significantly reduce her bills. In another month she'd be out of debt, two months from now she'd have a savings account.

How could a woman not fall in love with this guy? He never missed a trick. He saw everything that went on around him, rewarded people. Appreciated people.

She blinked back tears. "Thanks."

He rose from the table. "You're welcome."

She sat staring at the pay stub, a million things going through her mind. But no matter what direction her thoughts took they always came back to one simple fact. Jeb Worthington was a good man. And at Samuel's House she had realized that she loved him. He wouldn't have anything to do with her because he couldn't have children. But over the past weeks of emailing Macayla, her perspective of motherhood and mothering had changed dramatically.

But he didn't know that.

He walked to the door and for the first time Sophie realized how alone he looked, how deserted. Working for the kids at Samuel's House or on the ranch he was fine. At lunch and dinner with Slim, he was fine. But when he walked through the kitchen door, into rooms meant to be shared, the family room, media room—his bedroom—the emptiness of his life was obvious.

At the door, he turned and said, "I'll see you in the morning."

She nodded. But when the door swung closed behind him, her heart expanded in her chest. She couldn't stand to see him alone anymore. She loved him and she knew that if he'd give it half a chance he'd love her.

But she knew he wouldn't "give" it a chance. He wouldn't make a move. If anything was going to happen between them, it would be up to her.

Her mind made up, she rose from the kitchen table.

She was either about to change both of their lives or make the biggest mistake of her life.

An hour later, she stepped through the French doors out into the cool night air. Just as she expected, he was in the pool, cutting smoothly through the glistening water. His muscles rippled as he stroked, the faint sound of his movements cut through the silence.

He reached the edge of the pool, touched it and turned around again in one clean movement. Mesmerized, she watched, stripping her cover-up and dropping it to the chaise.

After a few seconds of watching him, her blood virtually sang through her veins. Physically he was perfect, but the arousal that shimmied through her took second place to the feelings swelling her heart. For two weeks she'd hidden the fact that she loved him. And it was time to quit pretending they could only be housekeeper and boss, when they could have so much more if he'd simply open his heart to the possibilities.

She knew there was only one way he'd accept her, a sacrifice. But tonight it seemed easy. They could have as many kids as they wanted. They simply wouldn't be biological children. But that was okay. There were plenty of kids like Macayla who needed her.

It was time to admit that they were meant to be more.

"Hey."

He stopped swimming, twisting to bring himself around to face her.

"Sophie?"

"Yeah."

He ran his hand down his face to scrape away the water. "What's up?"

"I just felt like a swim."

"Oh." He paused for a second as if needing to think that through then he said, "Okay." He hoisted himself out of the pool. "I'll leave."

"No!" Realizing how sharp her word had been, she took a light breath to soften it. "I mean… The pool's big enough for both of us. Why don't you stay?"

He yanked his towel from the chaise, dried his face and turned to her. "You know why."

She took a step closer. "Because we like each other?"

"Like isn't exactly the word I'd use."

She laughed. "All right. Maybe lust is a better word. But don't you think time's been working on changing that?"

She saw from the look on his face that he understood, but the way he drew in a long breath also told her that didn't make him happy. "Sophie, don't."

She caught his hand, yanked lightly in the direction of the pool. "Come on. Stay with me. Give us a chance."

He shook his head sadly. "It wouldn't work. And you know why."

"Yes, because you can't have children. And you don't want to deprive me." She sucked in a breath, steamrolling on before he could stop her. "But the past month with you and the trip to Samuel's House has changed things for me."

He caught her gaze. "What are you saying?"

"Well, you don't know this but I've been corresponding by email with Macayla."

"Sophie—" Her name came out as a growled warning.

But she laughed. "I know she's not anywhere near ready to go into a private home. I know she's still working things out. But someday she's going to be ready and when she is I'm going to be here for her."

"This isn't a good idea."

"Yes, it is," she insisted. "You might have read her file but her file doesn't tell the whole story. She had a normal life until her parents died. It's their deaths that made her so out of control. She only ran from two foster homes before they gave up on her and shipped her to Samuel's House. She's different from the other kids. More than anything else she needs to get over her parents' deaths. We could help her with that."

Jeb stepped back, away from her. "Don't."

"I know you're skeptical, but that's

actually good. You'd keep me grounded. When I'd want to adopt every child who came through the Samuel's House doors, you'd remind me that adoption isn't right for some of them. That they need their space. And the best thing we could do for them would be simply to be their friends. But Macayla is different."

He took another step back, didn't say anything.

She stopped the argument that instantly sprang to her head, finally realizing he wasn't disagreeing. He wasn't saying anything at all. "Jeb?"

He pulled in a breath, let his gaze ripple down the length of her body then squeezed his eyes shut. "If anybody could make me consider adoption, it would be you."

She would have laughed. Would have given into the glorious sensation that just having him look at her aroused, but she knew he'd only given her half a statement. He'd said if. *If* anybody could make him consider adoption…

If…

"What are you saying?"

"I'm saying that you're reaching for a solution I rejected long ago. I'm saying I've been down this road before and I know where it ends because I've been there."

Zoe. The little girl Jeb and his wife "almost" adopted. Pete hadn't known the whole story. He only had part. Even he admitted that.

"It was *you* who didn't want to adopt, wasn't it? Your wife would have taken Zoe, but you said no."

"I said no."

Her heart stopped and so did her breathing. She couldn't believe what he was saying. "But why?" She shook her head. "I don't get it."

"Of course, you don't! You're young and healthy and could have a hundred kids if you want. You have choices. I don't."

"So what you're really saying is that you're mad that you don't have choices. If you could have children, it wouldn't bother you to adopt."

"No... Yes..." He turned away. "I don't know."

"Oh, you do know. You know very well. You're standing your ground because you're mad."

"Yes, damn it!" He spun around to face her. "I spent my entire life on the outside looking in. Never enough. Lots of times the kid everybody pitied. I don't want to be pitied anymore.

I don't want to make excuses and take hand-outs of affection somebody tosses at me."

"I'm not tossing you a handout!"

"Aren't you?" He took a slow step toward her. His gaze rippled down her body, then strolled back to hers. "You came out here to seduce me. But instead of jumping into the pool, surprising me, catching me off guard, you called me out. Told me how you were going to compensate for my deficiency. Should I have been grateful? Were you expecting me to fall into your arms? Weep for joy? Tell you you could have me and everything I own because you were willing to sacrifice?"

"It wasn't like that." Shame burned through her. He made her sound so cheap. "You said you wouldn't have anything to do with me unless I knew what I was getting into. I thought that was what you needed to hear."

"Which just goes to show how little you know me." He laughed harshly. "You know what? It doesn't matter."

"Of course it does. We can work this out—"

"I don't want to work it out!" His angry shout reverberated through the quiet night. "Don't you get it? I want to be enough. I want a woman to come to me for me."

Sophie stared at him, working to understand what he was saying until she broke it down to the most simple terms. He wanted what she wanted. To be loved. Accepted. But where she would hug everybody in the world to her, hoping to find the person or people who could fill the void, he rejected everybody. Never believing he was really loved. He'd probably done this very thing to his ex-wife.

And now he was rejecting her.

No wonder he'd told her to stay away from him. She was a fixer. He didn't want to be fixed. They were the worst possible combination.

A lump formed in her throat. Tears filled her eyes.

Would she ever stop being the little girl trying to make a place for herself looking for love?

She turned and raced to the French doors. He didn't call her back.

Running back to her suite of rooms, she suddenly envisioned her and Jeb in the kitchen the following morning.

He wouldn't regret what he'd said, but he would regret hurting her. So he'd apologize, trying to make up for embarrassing her. Apologize for not loving her. Because he couldn't love and *she* was the one who was desperate for it, not him.

Humiliation tightened her chest. She ripped off her swimsuit, but rather than put on pajamas, she stepped into clean jeans and a T-shirt. She pulled things from the dresser drawers and closet, tossing them into her two suitcases. She now had thousands of dollars in her checking account. True, she'd wanted to pay off Brady's hospital bills with that money, but circumstances had changed.

She was done being the woman who tried to make everybody else happy. The fixer. The one who scurried to find a way. Only to be rejected every damned time.

This time she really would be on her own. For real. Not dependent on anybody for anything.

CHAPTER THIRTEEN

JEB walked into the kitchen at noon the following day expecting to smell lunch and finding the room cold and empty. The coffee he'd made at seven that morning sat on the still warm coffeemaker, smelling stale and strong.

"Sophie!" he called, striding through the downstairs, angrier than he'd been in a long time. He refused to take the blame for this. She'd started the episode the night before, offering something she really didn't want to give, and making him feel like a damned fool. Somebody so needy she had to give up what she wanted to make him feel okay.

Well, he wasn't having it. He was okay. Just the way he was. He didn't need anybody fixing him.

Assuming she was in her suite, maybe even holed up with Brady, he calmed himself before knocking on her door. It wouldn't do any good to yell. He'd yelled the night before but he'd been angry. Today he wanted to get them back to normal. A boss and house-keeper. A woman who needed him. Not the other way around.

When his knuckles hit the wood, the wood panel creaked and fell inward.

He frowned and peered inside. "Sophie?"

The room was dark and cool. The end tables were clear of the books and magazines she typically had lying around. "Sophie?"

Nothing.

He peered into the bedroom. The bed had been stripped. The crib was gone.

His heart stopped. "Sophie?"

He walked back to the sitting room, looking everywhere for any sign of an explanation but there wasn't even as much as a note.

She'd left him. No note. No goodbye.

He pulled in a breath. *She'd gone?*

He almost couldn't believe his eyes, but the argument they'd had the night before played over in his head and he realized some-thing he hadn't thought of before this. He'd been so angry, so caught up in the drama of his own troubles, that he hadn't really con-sidered her feelings. In the light of day, he'd figured she'd be mad, but he'd handled her anger before. Now, looking at the empty room, he suddenly realized he hadn't just rejected her the night before, he'd embarrassed her. And that was the one thing she couldn't handle.

Rubbing his hands down his face, he held back a sea of regret by deciding that maybe this was for the best. He couldn't be what she wanted. He didn't doubt that she believed she'd be okay with adoption, but he wasn't okay with it. She didn't realize that when he'd said he'd never be a father he meant it. He'd taken control by accepting who and what he was. It was the only way he could reconcile himself. So, no matter how much he liked and wanted Sophie and how much she liked and wanted him, he wouldn't deprive her.

This was for the best.

Turning, he strode to the door but a swatch of blue caught his gaze. He stopped. Brady's shiny blue bear lay on the floor. He stooped and picked it up. His eyes squeezed shut, but he willed away the pain, the regret, the sense of loss.

She'd gotten him to say and feel a hundred times more than what he knew was good for him. He was limited. Pretending he was okay—normal—when he wasn't, only made him feel worse.

Walking to the kitchen he opened the trash and tossed the bear inside. She wouldn't be back for it and hadn't left a forwarding address for him to mail it to her.

It was time to get on with the rest of his life.

Again.

Sophie awoke along a deserted stretch of highway with Brady crying in the car seat behind her.

She groaned at the stiffness of her body from sleeping sitting up. "Sorry, buddy." She'd left so late at night that around three o'clock, her eyelids had grown heavy and she'd known she had to stop to get some sleep. Brady slept soundly in the car seat, so she pushed her seat back and nodded off.

"I'll feed you and we can get back on the road."

Pulling a bottle from the cooler, she told herself not to think about Jeb. Not to wonder if he'd noticed her gone. Not to feel a spark of hope that he might come after her, look for her. Because she knew he wouldn't.

The embarrassment she'd felt—not from his rejection but from her stupidity in putting herself out to him—washed over her like a tsunami, but she decided the intense humiliation was a good thing. If she remembered the desperate expression on his face when he looked at Brady, her feelings softened. If she thought too long or too hard about what he said, she understood him. Because their battle was the same battle. Neither one of them really had anybody who loved them.

But if she remembered the humiliation, remembered that he refused her love, then she could get mad and probably even stay mad, and hopefully forget the crushing blow to her heart.

She fed Brady, forcing her mind to more pressing concerns. She had enough money for the first and last month's rent and even a security deposit, but if she didn't soon find a job she wouldn't have money for food. She drove the remainder of the way to California focusing her energy on the task at hand. She had to find work…and quickly.

Just over the border into California, she stopped at a diner and grabbed a copy of the local newspaper for something to read while she ate her late dinner. The paper automatically opened to the classified, she looked down and saw the ad for a two-bedroom apartment over a garage.

"I see you're looking at the ad for the Murphy place."

Smiling up at the waitress, Sophie closed the paper. "Not really. The paper just sort of opened."

The middle-aged woman handed her a menu. Dressed in a pink uniform with her hair pulled back in a severe bun, the waitress looked about fifty. "It's a great little apartment. Cheap, too."

"Yeah, well, it would have to be free next month because I don't have a job."

"What kind of work do you do?"

"I'm a maid."

The waitress sighed. "Too bad you're not a cook. I happen to need one."

"You own this place?"

She nodded. "Yes."

"I'm not a trained cook, but I *can* cook."

"We don't get too fancy here. It's not like you have to know anything more than eggs and beef stew."

Sophie laughed, but inside her heart stuttered. If she got this job she wouldn't have to go back to her parents and admit she'd lost her maid's job. She could rent the available apartment, live in an entirely different town, make new friends—make a new life.

"I get a little fancier than that."

"How fancy?"

"I make a wicked ziti."

The older woman laughed, extended her hand for shaking. "I'm Maggie. I lied when I said we didn't get too fancy because I was desperate. We need a cook so I was willing to take what I could get. But we're also just off the interstate and we get all kinds here. Truth is if you cook well, I'd happily make it worth your while to say."

"I cook well," Sophie said, deciding she might as well toot her own horn. If she was turning over a new leaf, no longer looking out for anybody but herself, she might as well start now.

Maggie slid onto the bench seat across the booth from her. "If we call this a job interview, dinner's on the house."

Jeb was standing by the sink trying to decide if he should grill hamburgers for himself and

Slim for lunch, when he realized he would have to break the news to his foreman that his wonderful dinners were now a thing of the past. Slim was going to throttle him.

Just as he thought that, Slim burst into the kitchen. "Clients are here." He stopped, glanced around. "Where's Sophie?"

Jeb shrugged. "No idea."

"She's gone?"

"Yep. And we're back to grilling burgers and steaks for every meal." He caught Slim's gaze. "You got a problem with that?"

Slim shook his head as if resigned. "Nope. I'm fine."

"Right." Jeb caught the backhanded implication that Jeb was the one with the problem, but he already knew that. Slim wouldn't say any more than he already had. He didn't have to. And Jeb wouldn't defend himself. He already had. Sophie was the one who'd thrown the monkey wrench into everything. It was time for his life and Slim's life and the ranch life to get back to normal.

"Let's go. Clients are waiting."

Two weeks later, Jeb got an urgent message from Pete Malloy. There was a problem at

Samuel's House that needed his attention.
Immediately.

His first thought was that something had
happened with Macayla, that Sophie
opening a line of communication and then
leaving had thrown her for a loop. But he
squelched it. She hadn't been that important. He wouldn't let her be that important.
Whatever was wrong with Macayla, one
way or another, he would make it right.
Without Sophie.

He napped in the plane and as always a car
awaited him at the airport. He jumped inside
and drove to Samuel's House.

Pete greeted him at the door. "Thanks for
coming."

"You said it was important."

Pete laughed. "It is. Come on."

He followed Pete to the dining room. At
the door, Pete more or less pushed Jeb in
front of him, and nudged him inside.

All sixteen of the Samuel's House kids
shouted, "Surprise! Happy Birthday."

Much to Jeb's own surprise, he laughed.
No one had ever thrown him a birthday party.

"Who is the squealer who told my
birthday? I didn't think anybody knew my

birthday." He really didn't. He'd never told anyone. Not even Slim.

Pete grimaced. "It was me."

Jeb turned to face him. "You? How did you know?"

Macayla stepped forward. "I'm not going to let Pete take the heat for me. I Googled you."

Jeb tried not to think of Sophie when he looked at her, but it was no use. This teenager with the big brown eyes, scraggly brown hair and nose ring had stolen Sophie's heart, changed how she felt, taken her away from Jeb.

He shook the thought from his head. No one had stolen Sophie. He'd let her go. That's how he had to remember it.

"You found my birthday through Google?"

She shrugged. "I have my ways." Then she turned away as Pete carried a big cake into the room.

The group of kids broke into a noisy rendition of Happy Birthday and Jeb stood speechless. He couldn't remember the last time anyone had told him happy birthday. Let alone made him a birthday cake.

Eating a piece of cake, he made his way through the group thanking them. Each of the kids had his or her own reason for being thrilled to throw the impromptu party. But Macayla had glossed over her part in things and had immediately begun talking about Sophie.

"She worries about you."

He turned away, pretending uninterest, but just as quickly turned back again. Was it so wrong to want to know she was okay? To at least know she had a job?

"How is she?"

Macayla shrugged. "Good. She loves California."

"Oh, she moved home?"

"Not hardly. Her parents like a visit now and again, but they're not much on having a baby around."

It broke his heart to think of Brady. Broke it again when he realized Sophie's parents treated the baby the same way they'd always treated her. Okay for sometimes, but not somebody they liked having around. Their own child and they neglected her. At least his parents had wanted him around.

"So where is she then?"

"Diner just outside the Nevada border."

"A diner?"

Macayla laughed. "She loves to cook."

He knew that, of course. He also knew she

wasn't a snob when it came to finding a job. All she ever wanted was a way to support her son.

And him.

She'd wanted him, too. She'd loved him. It was the first he'd let himself admit it, but he knew it as well as he knew his own name.

He tried to silence the little voice that nudged the memory of the night at the swimming pool to the front of his brain. She'd wanted to make love that night. She'd wanted to commit. To offer him a life and he'd thrown it all back in her face.

The pain of that washed over him. He hadn't meant any of what happened that night the way she'd taken it. He'd only been protecting himself. But he'd never before seen how protecting himself affected other people.

He'd embarrassed her. Humiliated her. Hurt her.

He told himself not to care. Not to worry. Not dwell on her. She'd be fine.

"Yeah, she lives in an apartment above a garage. Owned by some guy named Murphy. She says he's been coming on to her big time."

Macayla laughed but Jeb's blood boiled.

Though he could tell himself he didn't care that she'd moved on, he did care. He cared a lot.

"Is she making okay money?"

Macayla shrugged. "By your definition probably not. By my definition, she's got a place to stay and free meals for herself and Brady. She's doing great."

Macayla walked away casually, without offering the reassurances Jeb needed. Instead she'd planted seeds that caused him to go crazy with worry. For the next twenty-four hours he suffered with images of Sophie struggling. He pictured her apartment as being one room, with a tiny bath. He saw her eating one meal on her shift at the diner and going hungry the rest of the time.

Finally, when he couldn't take it anymore he called Macayla, swore her to secrecy and got the name of the diner where Sophie worked.

His hat low and sunglasses covering his eyes, he walked into the diner the next day. He didn't want to talk to Sophie. Simply wanted to know that she was okay. And—maybe—to check out the guy named Murphy. He strode to a booth in the back and when the waitress came with a menu, he ordered coffee.

* * *

"Oh, I am *sooo* glad you're here."

Sophie laughed at Maggie as she raced into the kitchen with an order. "I'm glad I'm here, too."

"No, I'm *seriously* glad," Maggie said, slapping her order receipt on Sophie's work table. "There's a cutie in the back booth ordered a Tex-Mex omelet. I'm not even sure I know what that is, let alone how to make it."

Maggie said Tex-Mex omelet and Sophie instantly thought of her first full day of working for Jeb. She told herself she had to stop letting her mind wander back. Jeb didn't want her. They were two different people. She'd always want to bring friends into her life. He'd always want to live in seclusion.

"I make a wicked Tex-Mex omelet."

"I know!" Maggie said, clapping her hands together with glee. "I was so lucky that you strolled into my diner!"

Sophie laughed, broke eggs into a bowl and began to make the omelet. When it was ready, Maggie hustled it out to the dining room.

A few minutes later, she returned, omelet in hand. "He says it's dry."

Sophie gaped at her. "Dry!" She'd never made a dry omelet in her life and after a night of Brady crying she wasn't in the mood for random complaints. She headed for the door. "Who is this guy?"

At the doorway she glared back into the dining room to the corner booth. When she saw Jeb her heart stopped. She ducked back into the kitchen.

"That's my old boss."

Maggie peered out into the dining room again. "That's the guy you used to work for? The mean old man."

Sophie cleared her throat. "I never really said he was old."

"Yeah, but you did say he was mean."

"He sent back the omelet, didn't he?"

Maggie laughed. "Yeah, but he's sweet as pie. Flirted with me the whole time he ordered."

Sophie whipped off her hairnet. "Don't let that fool you."

She grabbed the omelet and marched out into the dining room, shoving the plate under his nose. "You sent this back?" she asked, talking to the top of his hat because he hadn't taken it off.

Jeb's head came up. She saw her reflection in his sunglasses. "It was dry."

"If it's so dry, how about if you take off that hat and I dump it on your head?"

He pulled his sunglasses down. "You've gotten ornery."

"You always were ornery. So we're even."

She turned to walk away but he caught her hand. "We're not even close to even. You left without giving notice."

"Oh, I pretty much figured you knew I wouldn't hang around."

"You see, that's just it. I didn't figure you'd be leaving. I thought I'd at least have time to apologize."

"That's too bad, huh?"

"Well, that's sort of why I'm here."

"To apologize?"

He nodded. "And to say you were right."

"I'm always right." Except this time she wasn't sure what she'd been right about. "What was I right about?"

"Macayla doesn't belong at Samuel's House. I reread her file. Went a little farther back than the two foster homes she ran away from. Saw the part about her parents."

Her heart lifted. "So, you'd let me adopt her?"

He gave her an odd look, as if he was pondering something, then he smiled. "Why don't *we* adopt her?"

She took a step back. "Very funny."

"Not funny at all." His smile grew. "Actually it's the best idea I've come up with in a long time."

She slapped the omelet on the table, so she could put her hands on her hips. "What are you doing? She's already been through enough trauma! You can't promise her something you can't deliver."

"Oh, I'm delivering. My mind is absolutely made up. From where I sit it's you who's balking."

"I'm not coming back to be your maid."

"I didn't ask you to." He took off his sunglasses and caught her gaze. "I'd like you to be my wife."

Her heart stopped. Her breathing stuttered. "I... You..."

He pointed at the seat across from him. "Sit. Let me apologize. Let me tell you that I love you and I probably have loved you since the second day you were at my ranch."

She sat.

"I was afraid. And you were right. I was pushing people away. But you were also right when you said we handled the people in our lives differently. You gathered. I pushed." He reached across the table and caught her hand. "It doesn't seem to be working for either of us, so what do you say? Do you want to get married and work on meeting in the middle? Gather some people, push away others?"

The surprise of it shook her. Part of her wanted to shout yes and throw herself in his lap. The other part remembered the hurt, the humiliation of their last meeting. She swallowed. How could she trust him? "I don't know."

He tugged on her hand, forced her to look at him. "Do you love me?"

She nodded. "Yes. Unfortunately."

"Just what every man wants to hear."

"You're not an easy person to love." She didn't really mean that. He was probably the easiest person she'd ever met. She'd fallen in love with him in only a few weeks... Fear held her back. She'd held out her heart. He'd stomped on it. Now he expected her to believe he loved her...

He loved her.

Her head jerked up. "You love me?"

He nodded. "And want you to come home with me. We'll adopt Macayla. Give her the home she wants. I'll teach Brady how to rope and ride. And if you want more kids we'll look into adoption." He pulled in a breath. "Or, if you really want more of your own kids, we could look into that, too." He blew out his breath. "There's nothing wrong with you. You could have oodles of kids. And there are ways you could have them."

"But…"

"But nothing. They'd be yours but they'd also be mine because you'd be mine."

Tears filled her eyes, brimmed over, spilled down her cheeks. "That's a change."

He sat back, smiled wickedly. "I missed you."

She laughed through her tears.

"I've never been able to say that about anybody. My parents taught me not to depend on people, so I learned how to get by without everybody. You…" He shook his head. "It's not so easy to get along without you."

Without a word, Sophie got up from the booth and started to walk away. He caught her hand, tugging her back. "Where are you going?"

"To tell Maggie she needs to find a new cook."

He tugged again, brought her down to his lap. "Without answering me, first. I seem to remember putting a proposition on the table."

"I've decided to let you suffer for a few hours."

"While you pack?"

With a laugh, she nodded.

He shook his head. "You've gotta work on your punishment skills. The way I had it figured I'd have to camp out in this diner, work on you, maybe even seduce you into coming back with me for at least a week."

"You could still work on seducing me."

He lowered his head to kiss her. "Oh, yeah?"

"Yeah."

Then he kissed her and she knew everything was going to be okay. Not because he'd come back for her or because he agreed to adopt, but because he loved her. And she'd always heard people who genuinely loved each other could work anything out.

Now she knew they would. It was all a matter of finding the right person, the right love.

* * * * *

*Celebrate 60 years of pure reading
pleasure with Harlequin®!*

*Harlequin Presents® is proud to introduce
its gripping new miniseries,*
THE ROYAL HOUSE OF KAREDES.
*An exquisite coronation diamond, split as a
symbol of a warring royal family's feud, is
missing! But whoever reunites the diamond
halves will rule all....*

*Welcome to eight brand-new titles that
unfold to reveal the stories of kings and
queens, princes and princesses torn apart by
pride and power, but finally reunited by love.*

Step into the world of Karedes with
BILLIONAIRE PRINCE,
PREGNANT MISTRESS
Available July 2009
from Harlequin Presents®.

ALEXANDROS KAREDES, SNOW DUSTING the shoulders of his leather jacket and glittering like jewels in his dark hair, stood at the door. Maria felt the blood drain from her head.

"Good evening, Ms. Santos."

His voice was as she remembered it. Deep. Husky. Perfect English, but with the faintest hint of a Greek accent. And cold, as cold as it had been that awful morning she would never forget, when he'd accused her of horrible things, called her terrible names....

"Aren't you going to ask me in?"

She fought for composure. Last time they'd faced each other, they'd been on his turf. Now they were on hers. She was in command here, and that meant everything.

"There's a sign on the door downstairs," she said, her tone every bit as frigid as his. "It says, 'No soliciting or vagrants.'"

His lips drew back in a wolfish grin. "Very amusing."

"What do you want, Prince Alexandros?"

A tight smile eased across his mouth and it killed her that even now, knowing he was a vicious, arrogant man, she couldn't help but notice what a handsome mouth it was. Chiseled. Generous. Beautiful, like the rest of him, which made him living proof that beauty could, indeed, be only skin deep.

"Such formality, Maria. You were hardly so proper the last time we were together."

She knew his choice of words was deliberate. She felt her face heat; she couldn't help that but she damned well didn't have to let him lure her into a verbal sparring match.

"I'll ask you once more, your highness. What do you want?"

"Ask me in and I'll tell you."

"I have no intention of asking you in. Tell me why you're here or don't. It's your choice, just as it will be my choice to shut the door in your face."

He laughed. It infuriated her but she could hardly blame him. He was tall—six two, six three—and though he stood with one shoulder leaning against the door frame, hands tucked casually into the pockets of the jacket, his pose was deceptive. He was strong, with the leanly muscled body of a well-trained athlete.

She remembered his body with painful clarity. The feel of him under her hands. The power of him moving over her. The taste of him on her tongue.

Suddenly, he straightened, his laughter gone. "I have not come this distance to stand in your doorway," he said coldly, "and I am not going to leave until I am ready to do so. I suggest you stand aside and stop behaving like a petulant child."

A petulant child? Was that what he thought? This man who had spent hours making love to her and had then accused her of—of trading her body for profit?

Except it had not been love, it had been sex. And the sooner she got rid of him, the better.

She let go of the doorknob and stepped aside. "You have five minutes."

He strolled past her, bringing cold air and the scent of the night with him. She swung toward him, arms folded. He reached past her, pushed the door closed, then folded his arms, too. She wanted to open the door again but she'd be damned if she was going to get into a who's-in-charge-here argument with him. She was in charge, and he would surely see a tussle over the ground rules as a sign of weakness.

Instead, she looked past him at the big clock above her work table.

"Ten seconds gone," she said briskly. "You're wasting time, your highness."

"What I have to say will take longer than five minutes."

"Then you'll just have to learn to economize. More than five minutes, I'll call the police."

Instantly, his hand was wrapped around her wrist. He tugged her toward him, his dark-chocolate eyes almost black with anger.

"You do that and I'll tell every tabloid shark I can contact about how Maria Santos tried to buy a five-hundred-thousand-dollar commission by seducing a prince." He smiled thinly. "They'll lap it up."

* * * * *

*What will it take for this billionaire prince
to realize he's falling in love
with his mistress…?
Look for
BILLIONAIRE PRINCE, PREGNANT
MISTRESS
by Sandra Marton
Available July 2009
from Harlequin Presents®.*